THE BODY ON THE BEACH

AN ISLAND MYSTERY

ANNA JOHANNSEN

TRANSLATED BY LISA REINHARDT

Text copyright © 2017 by Anna Johannsen
Translation copyright © 2019 by Lisa Reinhardt

Previously published as *Der Tote im Strandkorb* by Edition M in Luxembourg in 2017. Translated from German by Lisa Reinhardt. First published in English by Thomas & Mercer in collaboration with Amazon Crossing in 2019.

Published by Thomas & Mercer in collaboration with Amazon Crossing, Seattle

www.apub.com

Amazon, the Amazon logo, Thomas & Mercer and Amazon Crossing are trademarks of Amazon.com, Inc., or its affiliates.

ISBN-13: 9781542003797
ISBN-10: 1542003792

Cover design by @blacksheep-uk.com

Printed in the United States of America

First edition

THE
BODY
ON THE
BEACH

Prologue

He's dead.

But his death was much too easy, overlooking the North Sea and the wide Kniepsand beach. I would rather he had died in a hole in the ground, dark and damp. Screaming with fear.

It was so easy. He had no idea, not even in his final seconds. I wish he'd known what he was paying for. That's the only thing I regret. Not his death — he brought that upon himself. He's responsible for how he met his end.

I hate him. His arrogance, his spiteful grin, his dead eyes. He is the perpetrator, not the victim.

I won't justify my actions. It was right and the only option.

He is dead.

But others still live.

It's a start. Nothing more.

1

Lena answered the call.

'Yes?' she said, not bothering to check the name on the display.

'Inspector Lorenzen, do you have a moment?' said Detective Superintendent Joachim Warnke. His tone was relaxed but Lena knew her boss wasn't asking.

'I'll be there in five,' she said coldly and hung up.

Their relationship had been less than cordial ever since Lena's stint under DSU Warnke's command during a special investigation. Unusually for him, he had led this investigation personally. An eight-year-old boy from Lübeck had been reported missing by his parents, but in spite of a large-scale search there was no trace of him. When there was still no ransom demand after four days, DSU Warnke had focussed the main search on known paedophiles in the Lübeck area. When Lena pointed out that the child's parents had been excluded as suspects far too quickly, her boss simply didn't want to know. And her own investigations had led nowhere. She'd had little chance of teasing out the contradictions in the parents' statements without the police force to back her. Despite her discretion in continuing her own research, a colleague had found out and within a few brief hours, she had been summoned to the super's office. She had received a black mark in her personnel file and been excluded from the remainder of the investigation. The missing boy was never found, and the unit had shrunk until the case was closed altogether.

Lena now knocked on the door and entered Warnke's office.

'Take a seat,' said her boss, gesturing at the chair in front of his desk. 'You grew up on Amrum, didn't you?' he asked.

'Born and bred. Why do you ask?'

'So you know the island well?' he asked, ignoring her question.

'I left the island after I finished high school. If I hadn't, I'd hardly be here – not as a DI, anyway. But you've read my personnel file.' Lena stressed the words *personnel file*.

Warnke pretended not to notice and continued, 'Any relatives on the island?'

'Yes,' said Lena, wondering where this strange conversation was leading.

'Ever heard of the children's home in' – he checked his notes – 'Norddorf?'

'Only from hearsay.'

'So you're not acquainted with or related to its director, Hein Bohlen?'

'Afraid not,' Lena said with growing irritation. 'Would you be so kind as to tell me what this is about?'

'Bear with me, Inspector.' Warnke's attempt at a smile failed. 'This Hein Bohlen was found dead at the beach two weeks ago. He was sitting in a beach chair – you know, one of those big wicker constructions with a roof and sides you can hire on most of the beaches up there. Our colleagues on Amrum called the local doctor who decided the cause of death was a heart attack. Apparently, he'd been treating Herr Bohlen for years. The doctor issued the death certificate and the case would have been open and shut.' DSU Warnke paused. 'Luckily, his next of kin demanded a post-mortem. To cut to the chase, someone raised doubts about the cause of death, and all of a sudden the local uniform agreed to class the case as suicide. By then, things had started to snowball and the body was brought to Forensics here in Kiel. They haven't finished examining it, but so far, the suspicion of foul play appears corroborated. In the meantime, the case was handed on to the next-higher authority and our colleagues in Flensburg have since discreetly asked the Criminal Investigation Department for assistance.'

'Discreetly?' asked Lena, surprised.

'Like I said, there are no definitive results from the post-mortem yet, only strong suspicions.'

'Which are?'

DSU Warnke swallowed. He knew he had to give Lena Lorenzen more than vague guesswork. 'Poison – a tropical poison, according to Dr Hinrichsen, and probably something that breaks down fast in the body, something difficult to detect. But yes, he believes he's found changes to the vital organs suggesting poison. He's contacted the Institute for Tropical Medicine in Hamburg, but it could be a while before we hear back. The poison in question may still be unknown to medical science. I told the people in Flensburg that I'm sending one of my men – or women, rather – to the island to investigate. They've assigned a young DS from their team to assist you. You have free rein.'

He slid a folder across the desk. 'Copies of all the documents.'

Lena groaned inwardly. Try as she might, she couldn't work it out. Why had Warnke picked her? It certainly wasn't because of his profound faith in her. Following the incident with the special investigation, she had nearly been demoted by one rank, until Warnke's retired predecessor, Enno Eilts, had intervened on her behalf and saved her from demotion or even worse. Something was seriously wrong with this assignment.

'You don't trust me,' Warnke said, 'and I don't blame you. Our relationship is somewhat . . . strained. Would that be fair to say?'

Now Lena was really confused. The superintendent had never spoken to her in this way before. He sounded open and honest, which Lena found extremely unsettling. What really lay behind this case?

'Yes, that would be fair to say,' she said eventually.

'My mother told me it always takes two to argue.'

Lena looked him in the eye. 'Your mother is a wise woman.'

'She was! Only I realised that much too late. Never mind.' He nudged the folder a little closer to Lena. 'What do you say? Don't you think the Amrum case is perfect for you?'

Why do I feel I can't trust him? Lena thought. *Something's not right.*

'I'm hardly in a position to turn down a case that's been assigned to me,' she said stiffly.

DSU Warnke raised an eyebrow. 'An interesting choice of words – inaccurate, however. You may decline, without consequences. I can put that in writing, if you like.'

Lena checked her watch. 'I'll take the late-afternoon ferry. Have the local police been informed?'

'They will be as soon as you walk out of my office.' He cleared his throat. 'Please report to me alone.' He handed her a sheet of paper. 'Only use this email address and phone number if you need to contact me.' Lena studied the note. Neither the address nor the number were familiar and she guessed they must be his personal contact details. 'Will you trust me for once?' he said.

'I'd like the assignment in writing.'

Warnke passed her a letter. 'I thought you might. Will this do?'

Lena skimmed through the text, nodded and rose. 'One report a day?'

Warnke stood up also and held out his hand in farewell. 'Yes, that'll do. Good luck, and look after yourself.'

Lena tried to keep her expression neutral. She'd have liked to tell him that this time round she'd certainly be playing her cards more closely to her chest than before. 'Can I count on you to have my back?'

'One hundred per cent.'

She nodded and headed for the door, then turned around one last time. 'I'll be in touch. Tomorrow night at the latest.'

Lena parked her work car, an older VW Passat saloon, outside the Institute of Forensic Medicine in Kiel, housed in one of the many unattractive red-brick buildings built since the war. Eighty per cent of Kiel had been destroyed in World War II because of its important naval port. At the time, the fjord of Kiel was the largest ships' grave-yard in the world with more than three hundred and fifty sunken vessels.

Lena had spent the last two hours going through the files and mak-ing several phone calls. She didn't like the thought of acting as Warnke's puppet and hated being no more than a pawn in a game of chess, wait-ing to be sacrificed for the king or queen at any moment.

Her first phone call had been to Enno Eilts, who had been just as puzzled as Lena at hearing the news.

'I have no idea what's going on,' he said. Lena could tell by his voice that he was worried for her. 'Warnke must be up to something. I can't imagine that your knowledge of the island is the only reason for recruiting you. There must be something else – he didn't give you any clues?'

'No, nothing. And I had the feeling that more questions would have been pointless.'

'He'll throw you to the wolves if it's in his own interest. It infuri-ated him when he failed to have you demoted that time. Warnke is a resentful and calculating man.'

'I won't make the same mistake twice,' Lena said. 'Do you think I should've turned him down?'

'He knew you'd accept. I bet it was part of his plan. The only advice I can offer is to watch your back. I'll keep an ear to the ground and let you know as soon as I learn anything.'

'Thanks, Enno.'

Their goodbyes had been heartfelt. Her next phone call had been to Leon, who wasn't particularly happy to hear her voice. They had known each other for almost three years, since he'd come into the firing line of an investigation and Lena had saved him from prosecution. Since then, Leon had helped her out now and again, gathering information fast and without a court order. His computer hacking skills had led to breakthroughs in several of Lena's cases. After some humming and hawing, he finally agreed to look into Hein Bohlen's email account.

Her third call had been to Ben, a colleague at the Flensburg constabulary who she had met at a conference. They didn't talk for long, and Ben promised to let her know if he heard anything. Two more phone calls later and she was finally on her way.

Lena now walked into the Institute of Forensic Medicine, hurried up to the first floor and along the corridor until she reached the door she was looking for. She knocked and went in.

'*Moin*, Lena – good morning!' came the greeting from the attractive, dark-haired woman behind the desk, along with a friendly smile.

Lena had rung Dr Luise Stahnke from her office and told her she was coming by. The two women had met three years ago in the course of a difficult investigation and had quickly become firm friends.

Lena gave Luise a hug and then seated herself in the chair in front of her desk.

'Let's take a look then,' Luise said, opening the folder Lena had slid across the desk.

Lena gave the pathologist a few moments to skim through the files, then asked, 'You've heard?'

Luise nodded. 'Yes. Sounds like a tricky and puzzling case. Jochen Hinrichsen and I talked about it the day before yesterday. He's convinced he'd have found traces of a tropical poison if the body had been brought to us sooner.'

'Do you think that's likely? I've never heard of such a poison.'

'Me neither, to be honest. But, as you know, that's not my area of expertise.'

'So what makes him think he would've found poison?'

'The damage to the heart, apparently. I don't want to bore you with the medical details, but to be honest, I didn't fully get it myself. I've never come across a case like this, but if there's anyone who knows anything about such things, it's Jochen. Guesswork won't hold up in court, however.'

'Any idea how fast-acting such a poison might be and how it would be administered?'

'Hard to say when we don't know exactly what toxin we're dealing with. It's too much speculation in my book. I'm sorry – I know that's no help at all to you, and you came here hoping for clues.' She sighed. 'Since Jochen couldn't find any needle punctures or anything else suggesting the poison was absorbed through the skin, chances are the victim took the substance orally.'

'How fast can a poison taken orally act?'

'Well, that's precisely what bothers me. A toxin needs to enter the bloodstream to take effect. And what's more, a poison of that type can usually be traced for years.'

Lena looked at her friend in confusion. 'I'm not sure I follow . . .'

'Jochen said it must be an entirely new or unknown poison, which can cause death even when taken orally and which breaks down almost instantly.'

'In other words, a super-poison for all potential murderers.'

'I know how it sounds, but Jochen seems to think it's a real possibility, which is why he called in our colleagues at the Institute for Tropical Medicine for support, though he said it'll take a while.'

'All sounds a bit mysterious, doesn't it? Hand on heart, Luise, what do you reckon to this?'

Luise Stahnke avoided the question. 'It's a pity Jochen isn't here or you could have asked him yourself. He's off on some professional development course in Munich.'

'I know. But that's not the only reason I came to you. So?'

Luise groaned. 'Honestly? It sounds like a load of old bull to me. Even if it's not my area of expertise, the theory's just too full of holes. I have no idea what's going on.'

'I feared as much. When can we expect results from the tropical institute?'

'A week at least, if not more.' Luise gave Lena a worried look. 'If the poison theory proves false, it probably won't turn out to be murder or manslaughter. Why did you take this assignment on? Isn't Warnke—?'

'I know, Luise. It was a gut decision. I accepted on instinct. Sorry, I must ask one more time: how long does it take for someone to die once a poison enters the bloodstream?'

Luise groaned again. 'God, you're like a dog with a bone – you just won't leave it alone, will you? All right, well . . . it could be anything from seconds to hours. I realise that's not much help to you.'

'What would you say is most likely?'

'The questions you ask! I'm a scientist, not a clairvoyant. If this new, mysterious poison actually exists, it could be anything. How could I possibly give an estimate?'

'And if you had to give one anyway, what would you—?'

'Not long,' Luise said, cutting her off. 'Ten minutes to half an hour. But like I said, this is pure guesswork and I'd never repeat it in public.'

'Thanks, anyway.'

'Wouldn't it be better to wait for the results from Hamburg?'

'I don't have the time. My investigation has to start right now. Every passing day destroys more clues – you know the game.'

'Amrum . . . Didn't you grow up there?'

Now it was Lena's turn to groan. 'Yes, I did.'

'You don't talk much about the island and your teenage years. Or do I have memory gaps due to our excessive alcohol consumption?'

'No, you don't.'

'Good!' Luise looked at her friend expectantly.

'Another time. I need to go if I want to catch the last ferry.'

The two friends hugged each other farewell and Lena promised to get in touch over the next few days.

2

'Lena Lorenzen.'

'Hello, DI Lorenzen. This is Detective Sergeant Johann Grasmann from Flensburg police.'

'You're up to speed?'

'Of course! I've organised accommodation on Amrum and studied the ferry timetable. What time would you prefer to depart?'

'We'll take the last ferry.'

'Roger that! I'll meet you by the dock at Dagebüll. Is there anything else you require of me?'

Lena grinned and was tempted to bark, 'Dismissed!' Instead she said, 'No thanks, all good. I look forward to working with you. See you later!'

'Yes, see you later, Detective Inspector.'

Lena sighed. Not a promising start. She certainly didn't need a chaperone or some earnest, blue-eyed youth. She only hoped Johann Grasmann was OK at research so she could keep him busy and out of her way.

She started up the engine and drove out of the city centre. A short drive later, she pulled up outside the attic flat she rented, opened the front door of the building and took the stairs, two steps at a time. Checking her watch, she unlocked the door to her flat, her heart thumping in her chest.

I must take up running again, she thought as she walked along the short hallway. Her living space was basically one large room built into the roof of the house. A wall partitioned off her bedroom space from the open-plan kitchenette and seating area. The large skylights gave the room the feel of a conservatory.

Lena grabbed her large duffel bag from a shelf and started to pack, then headed to the bathroom to fetch her toiletry bag. Pausing in front of the mirror, she inspected her appearance. As ever, her pale-blonde hair was tied back in a ponytail and she had gone without make-up. *Do I look older than thirty-three?* she asked herself and then shrugged. *Maybe I should go to the hairdresser when I get back.* She grinned at herself in the mirror. *Or better yet, a whole week at the health spa?*

Her phone buzzed on the way out. She checked the display. Joe, her colleague and kind-of boyfriend from the Kiel constabulary. They'd been seeing each other on and off for over a year. He'd texted asking if she wanted to meet him that evening at the Leierkasten, a small pub downtown. On her way down the stairs, she texted back that she'd be out of town for a few days. He replied with three question marks. 'Later,' she muttered, stashing her phone back in her pocket.

She climbed into her Passat and a few minutes later was on the main road to the autobahn. The steady hum of the engine put Lena into semi-autopilot. She adjusted the steering and kept a close eye on the congested traffic, but all the while her thoughts remained focussed on the case.

She still couldn't work out why DSU Warnke had landed her with this assignment. It couldn't just be her upbringing on Amrum. There was something not quite right about Warnke's sudden change from condescending superior to kindly colleague bestowing a seemingly important task upon her. He knew full well that Lena didn't trust him and that he couldn't count on her loyalty. Had he set her up to fail on purpose? But why?

Her phone rang and she answered it using the hands-free.

'It's me,' Joe said. 'Where are you off to?'

'Amrum,' said Lena, trying to keep her tone neutral. She hated it when Joe checked up on her.

'Work or pleasure?'

'What do you think?' replied Lena grumpily. She hadn't told him much about her past, but enough for him to realise that she wasn't off for a summer holiday on the island.

'All right, take it easy. The body on the beach? I thought that was—'

'You're well informed.'

'Woah, Lena. It was front-page news. What's the matter?'

'I need to focus on driving. Can we talk later?'

He sighed. 'OK, I understand. Keep in touch. Please?'

'Catch you later,' Lena said and hung up.

She wondered why Joe always seemed to call at the worst possible moment. Now he'd be mulling over their brief conversation for hours. He'd been talking about them moving in together for months, and twice already he'd asked her to visit his parents in Frankfurt. Either he wasn't put off by her dismissive attitude or he was drawing the wrong conclusions – and yet he was trained to read people. Right now, she wanted neither to move in with Joe nor visit his parents, and least of all to have to justify herself for it.

Lena crossed from the A210 on to the A7. Just before Flensburg, she would need to leave the autobahn for the highway that led right across Schleswig-Holstein, from the Baltic Sea to the North Sea on the other side.

Until just a few weeks ago, the landscape bordering the Baltic Sea had been bright yellow with flowering fields of rapeseed. Now, in mid-June, temperatures were pleasantly warm at around twenty degrees.

Lena loved going for walks along the cliffs, with the wide-open space of the Baltic Sea to one side and blossoming rapeseed and green meadows to the other. Here, she could walk for hours, letting her thoughts drift. She rarely asked Joe to join her.

Lena knew she couldn't string him along for much longer. Even though Joe was only one year older than her, he was ready to settle down. They had never talked about marriage and children, but Lena was sure this was his dream. And she felt less than certain about being the one to fulfil that dream. She winced every time he spoke about love. Once again she asked herself if they really had a future together.

On paper, Joe was the ideal man for her. He was a good listener, he was kind and he didn't need to be the centre of attention. He was understanding of her huge need for space and the fact that she only wanted him close some of the time. Why couldn't things just stay that way forever?

An hour and a half later, Lena sighted the ferry dock at Dagebüll and, next to an old Golf, a young man who seemed to be on the lookout for someone. She pulled up beside him and let down the right-hand window.

'You don't happen to be a policeman, do you?' asked Lena with a serious face.

The young man blushed. 'Detective Inspector Lorenzen from CID Kiel?'

'I couldn't have put it better myself.'

Johann Grasmann stepped closer to the window. Lena judged him to be around twenty-five. His thick, dark hair was combed back neatly and he was freshly shaved. He wore black jeans, a tailored suit jacket of the same colour and, all in all, Lena thought he looked a little lost.

'I'm—'

'I know. I suggest you leave your car here and we carry on in mine.'

Johann Grasmann turned towards his Golf as though bidding it farewell. Turning back to Lena once more, he nodded diligently. 'OK, fine. I'll just get my things.'

Johann sat in the passenger seat in silence as they drove on to the car deck of the ferry, his briefcase on his knees.

'Looks like we're stuck with each other for a few days,' Lena said. 'First names will be easier.' She parked in the designated spot, turned off the engine, and applied the handbrake before holding out her hand. 'Agreed?'

He nodded, embarrassed, but took her hand and said, 'Johann.'

Lena grinned. 'I know. Lena. But you already knew that.' She opened her door. 'I need some fresh air. How about you fill me in upstairs?'

A short while later, they were standing by the railing on the upper deck. The ferry had set off and was gaining speed.

Lena inhaled deeply. 'The North Sea breeze has its own particular charm.' Johann remained silent, apparently considering her comment. 'Don't you think?'

'I'm not sure. I've never thought about it.'

'Where did you grow up?'

He cleared his throat. 'On the Lower Rhine. Near Kempen.'

Lena grinned. 'Not a lot of wind but rather Catholic?'

Johann scratched his head. 'Yes, I'd say you've hit the nail on the head.' He grinned. 'But once a year, at carnival, it's where everyone wants to be.'

'Oh, that's right, I'd forgotten about that.' Lena tilted back her head and took in another lungful of air. 'OK, let's talk about the case. I left as soon as I got the assignment. Can you bring me up to speed?'

'Yes, ma'am!' replied Johann eagerly.

Lena shot him a stern look. 'A little less of the formal, if you will.'

'I'm sorry, but—'

'It's all right. Anything useful in the files? I only skimmed through them in Kiel. I'll take a closer look tonight but, until then, can you give me an overview?'

'Of course,' Johann said, straightening up a little. 'Our victim, Hein Bohlen, was fifty-one years old, a social educator and caregiver and director of the children's home in Norddorf. Born in East Friesland, studied at Emden University, and eventually worked in homes near Leer and other cities throughout northern Germany. Fourteen years ago he bought a house on Amrum and converted it into a children's residential care home, which opened a year later. The home takes up to fifteen boys aged from five to sixteen and employs six women. One of them is the victim's wife, also a social educator and caregiver. There are two other full-time employees: an on-site teacher and the cook. Then there is a cleaner and two further casual staff. Hein Bohlen had no convictions but I don't know if he ever had any run-ins with the law as a youth. Those files are either destroyed or under lock and key.' Johann Grasmann looked at his notes and continued. 'Bohlen's GP classed the cause of death as a heart attack, but results from the subsequent autopsy suggest it was poisoning. We're still awaiting final results.'

He paused briefly and seemed to choose his next words carefully. 'It would appear that the local uniforms didn't do themselves too proud. You can imagine what it's like in such a small community: everyone's related or at least acquainted with each other, so a natural death is much more convenient for everyone, especially since the GP spoke of a previous illness and issued the death certificate without hesitation. So now it's up to us to start from scratch.' Johann sighed theatrically. 'No suicide letter was found, and the brief statements from the wife and the two employees don't suggest foul play. The victim was popular and involved in his community – he was a member of the church choir and the sports club. I reckon we should start with the doctor and carry on from there with the wife and staff.'

'Do we know where Hein Bohlen got the money for the house and the renovations?'

Johann scanned his notes. 'No, or at least there's nothing on file. But there'd have been no obligation to register that information. He probably just got a bank loan.'

'Even fourteen years ago, house prices on Amrum were horrendous. Considering how big the house must be, we're easily talking a million or more. No bank would have lent him that sort of money without a considerable deposit.'

Johann made a note. 'That should be easy enough to find out. I'll pass it on to Flensburg in the morning.'

'Don't. If anyone knows, it'll be the nearest tax office. We'll ask them. Speaking of Flensburg, how come they picked you to assist me?' Lena asked abruptly.

Johann looked bewildered for a moment. 'Three of my colleagues are on leave, another got injured playing sports at the weekend and is in hospital, two more are—'

'Fine,' Lena said, cutting him off. 'We'll return to that question another time. What's your view on the case?'

'Going by the evidence—'

'I mean, what is your gut feeling?'

Johann sighed and shrugged his shoulders.

'Then we're on the same page,' Lena said in reply. 'Like I said, I'm going to take a proper look through the files tonight and we'll start right from the beginning tomorrow. To us, Hein Bohlen's body was found only a few hours ago.'

The ferry was on the open sea now. To their right, they could see Föhr in the distance, where the ferry would make a stop at Wyk before continuing to Wittdün on Amrum. Lena tried to work out how long it had been since her last visit to the island. Was it five or six years? Her Aunt Beke's husband had died and Lena had gone to the funeral. She couldn't help but smile when she thought of her favourite aunt. Beke Althusen was her mother's older sister by nine years. She and Lena had always been close. Beke visited her niece in Kiel at least once a year and they spoke on the phone every few weeks.

'I think we stop at Wyk on Föhr in about fifteen minutes,' Johann Grasmann said, looking out toward the island. 'And then on to Amrum.'

Lena was startled from her thoughts. 'You've never been to Amrum or Föhr?'

'No, sadly not. After graduating from police training college I applied for a position in Flensburg. That was four years ago. I like to holiday in Scandinavia – Sweden, Norway. Great places for hiking in spring and autumn.'

'I was born and raised on Amrum. I'm sure they told you.'

'Yes, the boss did mention it.'

'Did he warn you about me?'

Johann shrugged.

'And?' asked Lena.

'Not explicitly,' Johann said eventually, looking very uncomfortable.

'Well, really!' said Lena with a grin. 'I thought my reputation was worse than that.' She decided to ask her colleague the same question again in a few days' time.

'We're staying at a kind of community guest house,' Johann said, eager to change the subject.

'Not bad! How did you manage that?'

He laughed. 'I can be very tenacious, or at least my mother reckons so. Normally, the house is reserved for guests of the community. The last lodger was an author who stayed for six months. Kitchen, bathroom, two bedrooms, and even a small office – exactly what we need. And it's in Norddorf.'

Lena nodded. 'Well done. I thought we'd need to camp out in some musty old hotel.'

Johann beamed at the praise.

Lena nudged him with her shoulder. 'Looks like you and I might yet turn into a dream team, eh?'

3

'Lena! How lovely to hear from you,' Beke said. 'How are you?'

'Good, thanks, Beke.'

'The connection is terrible. Where are you?'

'On the ferry, not far from Wittdün.' Beke seemed too surprised to answer. 'I'll be working on the island for a few days.'

'Hein Bohlen?' asked Beke.

'I can't say. You know that.'

'I know, *deern*, and it doesn't matter. The main thing is, you're here. Why don't you stay here with me? I've got plenty of room.'

'Thanks, Beke. My colleague and I already have somewhere fixed up through work, but I'll try to get away for a couple of hours tomorrow to come and say hi. Would that suit you?'

'As if you have to ask! Of course it does.' She cleared her throat. 'Does your father know you're coming?'

'No.'

'But don't you think—?'

'Absolutely not. I feel exactly the same as I did before. Beke, we're about to dock and I have to get back to my car. I'll be in touch, promise.'

'All right, *deern*. Look after yourself. There's all kinds of talk.'

'Will do, Beke. See you tomorrow.'

Lena, who had gone to the next deck down to make the call, slipped her phone back in her pocket and made her way to the Passat. Johann had gone to the bathroom.

As she sat at the steering wheel waiting for the bow to open, for the first time since she'd started this trip to Amrum Lena's gut clenched, as it had done on so many trips in the past. How many times had she travelled between the two ports? She must have spent hundreds of hours on ferries during her school years. She had studied for tests on ferries, done her homework and filled one diary after the other. She assumed they were still hidden in the attic of her childhood home.

'We can go,' said Johann, rousing her from her thoughts.

She started up the engine and followed a blue Volvo off the ferry. A police car was parked at the side of the road that led from the ferry terminal to the centre of the village. A policeman in uniform stood next to the car.

'Welcome committee?' asked Lena. 'Did you call ahead?'

'They asked me to. I thought—'

'Let's make one thing clear: if you want to work with me, you must always tell me every tiny detail to do with the case.'

'I didn't mean—' Johann broke off when he saw Lena's look.

Eventually, he muttered, 'OK', and wound down the window when they reached the policeman. The man – mid-fifties, beginnings of a paunch, red hair – smiled frostily.

'DS Johann Grasmann, Flensburg police,' Johann said by way of introduction and then turned briefly to Lena. 'And this is DI Lorenzen from Criminal Investigation.' Johann looked out of the window again and asked, 'Did we speak on the phone?'

The police officer shook his hand. 'Sergeant Walter Reimers. I'm in charge of the Amrum police station. I suggest we sit down together and discuss our line of approach. Follow me. It's only a short distance to Nebel.'

Johann turned to Lena. She gave a small nod. 'OK,' he replied.

Reimers seemed satisfied. He climbed into his car and pulled out without indicating. Johann didn't dare speak until they were on the open road leading to Nebel. 'We can't entirely avoid working with our local colleagues.'

'It wasn't about that,' Lena said. 'I want to be prepared, and to be fully prepared I need to know everything. And now this sergeant wants to stick his oar in.'

'But we're only going to have a chat about things.'

'Wait and see,' Lena said, following the police car off the main road. A short while later, they pulled up in a courtyard encircled by trees. Lena was familiar with the inconspicuous brick building that housed the police station.

'Did you know that – technically speaking – the Amrum police station was dissolved two years ago and is now merely a branch of the Föhr police, DI Lorenzen?' asked Johann.

Lena rolled her eyes and shook her head. 'Don't you worry, my dear colleague, I have done *some* homework. And we need to work on that first-name basis, OK?'

Reimers was waiting at the door. 'Welcome to our hovel, such as it is,' he said, a strained smile on his face. 'Come on in!' He led them through to his office and asked Lena and Johann to take a seat, gesturing towards the two chairs in front of his desk.

'One of my men is on patrol and the other's knocked off for the day. Our core team consists of two constables and my humble self, along with an extra two constables from the mainland in peak season. Can I get you something to drink? Coffee, tea, water?'

'Thanks, but that won't be necessary,' Lena said.

'All right. I heard you've found decent accommodation in Norddorf. Don't hesitate to ask if you need anything.' He grinned. 'Your friendly local police – always ready to help and support.'

'Thanks, we'll be fine,' Lena replied with a professional smile.

'Good, that's good,' Reimers replied awkwardly. 'Needless to say, I'm at your disposal any time regarding the case. I know the island well and' – he paused for effect – 'I'd imagine my company might be quite useful. People here can be rather stand-offish, especially with strangers . . .'

Lena rose to her feet. 'If we need assistance, we know where to find you.'

Reimers looked irritated. 'As you wish.' He stood up also and held out his hand to Lena. 'Looking forward to working with you.' He nodded at Johann and led the way to the door.

Back in the car, Johann asked, 'What was that all about?'

'An overly welcoming sergeant with sweaty palms,' said Lena, driving back out on to the main road.

'Some information about the island?' asked Lena, and continued without waiting for a reply. 'You've already seen Wittdün. The village came into existence alongside the ferry terminal; the port used to be farther north in Steenodde. Here we find ourselves in Nebel, which means *fog* but has nothing to do with the fact that it's often foggy. As you can see, there are still plenty of old Frisian houses with thatched roofs in Nebel, not all of them actually old, but that's a different story. Sailors from Amrum travelled all around the world, many of them on whaling missions. The most successful among them – captains, mainly – competed with one another over who could build the most beautiful house here in Nebel, while the less successful stayed out at sea – and that's how Nebel gradually grew bigger. The northernmost village is Norddorf. It's the most touristy of all, with restaurants, cafés, hotels, B&Bs – you name it. Luckily, Amrum folk kept large-scale tourism out for as long as they could, which is why you won't find any architectural eyesores like you do on Sylt. The biggest attraction here is the Kniepsand, a huge beach on the west coast, almost a mile wide in places. It's actually a sandbank. You'll see it tomorrow.'

They were nearing the next village and passed a sign reading *Norddorf*. Johann entered the address of the guest house into the satnav and started the navigation.

'Just to be sure,' he said. 'And we need to pick the keys up too.'

Their first destination was a small café in the heart of the village. Johann got out and returned a few minutes later. He handed Lena a key. 'I asked for two, so we can be independent of each other.'

Lena started the engine and was directed through Norddorf by the pleasant voice from the satnav. Eventually, they reached an intersection; straight ahead of them a dirt road led into the conservation area. They turned left and, as they passed the last house, the voice told them to take a sandy road. A minute or two later, Lena drew up outside a small Frisian house with a thatched roof.

'Nice,' she said, switching off the ignition. 'And so close to the beach. I hope you packed your trunks?'

'Is the North Sea warm enough yet?' Johann asked doubtfully.

'Depends on how sensitive you are. When I was a child, we went swimming in May if the weather was fine – never for long, though,' she said, grinning, and opened her door. 'Shall we?'

The red-brick house with its white-painted wooden window frames looked newly renovated. Lena remembered that an old woman with no relatives had once lived here. In such cases the property passed into the ownership of the state. A wise decision, thought Lena, as they entered the house. The interior had also been restored with a light hand, pre-serving the character of the old place. Apart from a kitchen, there was a kind of study as well as a small sitting room.

Johann left the larger bedroom to Lena, which she accepted with-out comment.

'I need to stretch my legs,' she said. 'I'll see you in the morning. Seven o'clock?'

'Sure, no problem.'

'If you're hungry, I recommend the Strandhalle beach restaurant. Go back to the road and you'll be there in two minutes.'

He looked at her expectantly.

'The salty North Sea breeze and a walk on the Kniepsand will do me,' she said, laughing. 'I need to watch my figure.'

She closed her bedroom door and opened the window. It was a good-sized room. Aside from the double bed and a large wardrobe, there was a seating area with two armchairs and a small table. Lena put down her bag, pulled the P2000 Heckler & Koch from its holster and placed it on the bedside table before sinking down on to the mattress and gazing up at the ceiling.

The oppressive feeling hadn't let up during the drive across the island. But now, in this entirely unfamiliar room, she started to relax a little. Lena hoped a walk on the beach would do her good. If there was anything about Amrum she'd missed, it was the Kniepsand, with its endlessly wide expanse of beach.

She checked her phone. It was just past six o'clock. There wouldn't be many holidaymakers left on the beach at this hour, and if she avoided the Strandhalle, she could walk for hours without running into anyone. She leapt off the bed and walked out of the room.

'Lena?' came a male voice from the door.

She turned. Erck had hardly aged in the fourteen years since their last meeting, except that the lanky body of the youth had given way to a stronger, more manly stature. His eyes hadn't lost the glow that had bewitched her all those years ago.

Erck had seemingly appeared from nowhere. She guessed he must have been in one of the beach huts they'd passed on their way. Those huts – technically illegal – were tolerated by the council as long as they were entirely constructed from driftwood and other beach detritus. Most of the huts were creative constructions that had to be resurrected each summer. Some beach hut builders buried their materials in the autumn and dug them out again in early summer.

'I was helping friends rebuild their beach hut,' Erck said in response to Lena's look of surprise. 'Since when are you back on the island?'

Lena slowly recovered from the initial shock of seeing him. 'Not very long,' she murmured.

'I can't believe we ran into each other right away,' Erck said with excitement. He stepped towards her to take her in his arms. 'Don't be angry with me,' he whispered, 'but I need to do this.' After a few moments, he took a step back and studied her face. 'You're even more beautiful than you used to be.'

Lena smiled in spite of herself. 'And you're an even bigger charmer than you were fourteen years ago.'

'Has it been that long?'

Lena didn't reply. At least Erck didn't seem to bear her any grudge. Her sudden departure from Amrum had been her only option back then.

'How long are you staying?' asked Erck, still looking amazed at Lena's sudden reappearance.

'I'm not sure.'

'Has something happened to your father? No, I would have heard. Or Beke?'

'No, I'm here for work.'

'Hein Bohlen? Are you investigating his death? Strange, I thought you were with the CID in Kiel. Or—'

'I am,' she said.

He raised an eyebrow. 'Sounds serious. I heard via the grapevine that it might not have been a heart attack after all. But . . .' He paused. 'Murder? Here on Amrum?'

'I can't talk about it.'

'Yes, of course. Sorry. But . . . are you going to have any spare time? Have you eaten? We could—'

'Erck, I'm sorry. I need to go over the files.'

'Dammit.'

Lena could tell how disappointed he was.

'How about tomorrow or the next day?'

Lena hesitated. 'I don't know if that's such a good idea . . .'

Their eyes met.

'The Lena I knew wasn't afraid of anything. What's the worst that could happen? I'm sorry, but you won't get away from me that easily again. Tomorrow or the next day? I'd prefer tomorrow.'

Lena sighed. 'I'll think about it, OK?'

Erck pulled a pen from his pocket, grasped her hand, and scrawled a number on her palm. 'Call me?'

Lena hesitated for a few moments, then nodded.

4

Lena walked into the small kitchen the next morning to find Johann at the stove, pouring water into the coffee filter. A basket with four bread rolls sat on the table, together with butter, jam, ham and cheese.

'I went shopping last night,' Johann said when he saw Lena looking at the table.

'*Moin, moin,*' she said in greeting and sat down at the table. 'Looks good.'

Johann dumped the filter in the sink and brought the pot of coffee to the table.

'Black, thanks,' Lena said with a smile.

Johann sat down too. 'You do eat breakfast, don't you?'

'I will today,' she replied, helping herself to a roll.

'So what's the plan?' asked Johann once he'd poured coffee for them both.

'Hein Bohlen was found by two holidaymakers. I'm guessing they've left the island by now.'

'As indeed they have – I checked yesterday. They live in Hanover. I asked the local station for support. One of my former classmates from college is a constable there and he was going to pay them a visit and get back to me today.'

'That's great – only, what would the poor people from Hanover have said if I'd sent someone along too?'

'OK, my mistake,' Johann replied after a brief pause, a blush spreading across his features. 'I should have let you know yesterday.'

'Everything's hard at the start, like my Aunt Beke always says.'

◆ ◆ ◆

Johann punched the address of the children's home into the satnav.

'I think I can manage without that,' Lena said and started the car.

The drive through Norddorf didn't make her feel as uncomfortable as it had the day before. Erck popped into her thoughts. She'd saved the number he'd written on her hand on to her phone. Her thoughts had kept drifting to her first love while she was studying the case file last night. Fourteen years ago, she'd begged him to come with her, even though she knew how attached he was to this patch of dirt in the middle of the North Sea. A week before she was due to leave Amrum for good, he'd told her amid tears that he was going to stay on the island.

'Inspector – I mean, Lena, what do you think about Sabine Bohlen?' asked Johann as they drew near the children's home.

'Well, she asked for a post-mortem. You wouldn't do that if you were the murderer, would you?'

'Yes, but . . .'

'Go on.'

'She might have been afraid the truth would come out later so did it as a measure of precaution, so to speak? And the likelihood of a post-mortem actually happening seemed very small.'

That's precisely what had been bothering Lena ever since her conversation with DSU Warnke, but not so much because of the widow herself. After the death certificate was issued, together with the plausible explanation of a previous illness, there should have been no reason to conduct a post-mortem, but nonetheless the Flensburg headquarters had taken the initiative. Lena wondered whether the reason was indeed

Sabine Bohlen's doubt over the cause of her husband's death, or if there was something else.

'We'll see. Did you call ahead, Johann?'

He nodded. Lena could tell he still wasn't entirely comfortable with them addressing each other by their first names.

She parked in front of the children's home. The two-storey brick building with its black roof tiles lay east of Norddorf. Lena estimated that someone could walk briskly over to the mudflats on the eastern shore in a little over two minutes.

The two detectives climbed out of the car. The door opened as they walked up towards the entrance, and a woman of around forty with short black hair came out to greet them. She was, Lena guessed, around five foot two, and she wore jeans and a baggy grey shirt which concealed her figure.

Lena held out her hand to the woman. 'Good morning. I'm Detective Inspector Lorenzen, CID Kiel, and this is DS Grasmann from Flensburg.'

'Sabine Bohlen. Please come in.'

They walked down a long corridor with numerous closed doors. A metal sign reading *Management* hung on the last door. The office was plain, with an old wooden desk and a table with four chairs.

'Take a seat,' said Sabine Bohlen, waiting for Lena and Johann to sit down. 'Can I offer you something to drink?'

'No, thanks, we've just had coffee,' Lena replied.

Sabine Bohlen didn't move, gazing in turn at Johann and Lena, so Lena pulled back a chair and gestured for her to sit.

'We're investigating the possible murder of your husband,' Lena said calmly.

'Murder? He didn't . . . ?' asked the woman.

'We're not a hundred per cent sure yet, but there is some evidence to suggest that he didn't die of natural causes. We'd like your help in reconstructing your husband's movements on his final day. Let's start in the morning. What time did you get up?'

Sabine Bohlen hesitated briefly, then she sighed and said, 'Same as always. It would have been around half past five. I get breakfast ready for the children, which takes a while. Hein goes . . .' She swallowed. 'Hein used to go to the office, start up the computer, check his emails, and so on. Around half past six he'd wake the children and give me a hand. That Tuesday was like any other day . . .' She stopped.

'So you got out of bed together . . .' Lena said encouragingly.

'We sleep – used to sleep – in separate bedrooms. I'm a very light sleeper and Hein used to go for walks late in the evening, and sometimes he snored. Not every night, but like I said, I'm a very light sleeper.'

'So the first time you saw your husband that day was in the kitchen?'

'Yes, I'm fairly sure – the same as every day. Of course, sometimes we ran into each other on the way to the bathroom, but that day . . . No, I'm pretty certain that I only saw him once he'd woken the children.'

'And then he helped you with breakfast?'

'No, not that morning. He said there was something he needed to do and went to his office.'

'Do you know what he meant?'

'No. I assumed it was paperwork – there's always paperwork to sort out. The authorities swamp us with forms and inquiries. The tax office automatically assumes institutions like ours are tax evaders, and the council continuously comes up with ridiculous and time-consuming new regulations. Not to mention the school – looked-after children always get branded as trouble-making welfare cases, no matter how hard the little ones try.'

Sabine Bohlen glared at the detectives indignantly, as though they were responsible for the unfair treatment of her wards. Her face had turned red. Then she seemed to remember who she was talking to. 'I'm sorry. I'm a nervous wreck at the moment.'

'Of course. We understand,' Johann said in gentle tones. 'Please, tell us what your husband did that morning.'

Sabine Bohlen took a deep breath. 'Yes, what did he do? First he drove the children to school and the three little ones to kindergarten. We've been driving them ever since a group of youths ambushed our kids on their way to school.' She sighed. 'When he returned – wait, no, he didn't – he went straight to the supermarket and didn't come back. We handle the cooking ourselves, which means we have to get groceries in every other day. That usually takes between one to two hours. And then . . . he had an appointment, but don't ask me who with. Most likely with our accountant Tamme Lüschen in Wittdün, but I'm not a hundred per cent on that. I guess Hein was back in time for lunch. And then—'

Johann asked for the name of the supermarket and whether he could have the receipt. Sabine Bohlen nodded.

'You can't say for certain whether he came back here after his appointment?' asked Lena Lorenzen.

'All the days run together in this place. I'm sorry. Why do you want to know?'

'Frau Bohlen,' said Johann in the same friendly tone as before, 'we're at the very start of our investigation and it's impossible to tell yet which of the many details may prove significant further down the track.'

Sabine Bohlen gave him a grateful look. She stood up, fetched a piece of paper from her desk and handed it to him. 'You asked me on the phone to note down my husband's friends and associates. I hope I haven't forgotten anyone.'

Johann Grasmann took the list. 'Thank you very much. This will make our job so much easier. Now let's return to your husband's day. We'll leave it open for the moment as to whether he was back for lunch or not. You said he took the children to school and kindergarten. Did he pick them up at the end of the day as well?'

'I don't think so,' Sabine Bohlen said. 'Isabel must have done it that day. We have a minibus for that purpose.'

'Isabel?' asked Lena.

'Our in-house teacher and caregiver, Isabel Müller. She replaced Anna about six months ago.' Frau Bohlen wrinkled her nose. 'Anna quit without giving any notice. We were awfully lucky to find Isabel.'

'So . . . your employee picked up the children,' Lena said. 'And that afternoon – was your husband back?'

'I can't tell you with a hundred per cent certainty. He's usually here because homework time is the most challenging part of our day. Completing high school is the single most important factor in breaking the vicious cycle. Most of our children come from broken families – drugs and alcohol, abuse and unemployment.'

'So your husband's normally home in the afternoon?' asked Lena.

'Yes, of course, that's what I just said,' Sabine Bohlen snapped. 'Weren't you listening?'

'Of course DI Lorenzen is listening,' Johann said soothingly. 'It's simply part of our job to ask for details and make absolutely sure we've understood everything correctly.'

'I'm sorry. It's like I said – my nerves.' Sabine Bohlen closed her eyes for a moment. 'Where were we?'

'The afternoon,' Johann said. 'How long is homework time usually?'

'We try to be finished by four. The children need time to play and develop their own interests. We want to prepare them for the real world out there and that often has very little to do with school. We try to get them involved in looking after the house and the garden – on a voluntary basis, of course. Taking responsibility for oneself is very, very important to us. They need to decide for themselves how they want to spend their free time and what they might volunteer for. We call it free project work.'

'I read that you studied the theory of social education,' Johann said. 'I think it's most impressive how you offer the children an environment that many kids living with their parents wouldn't be receiving.'

Sabine Bohlen looked pleased. 'Yes, well, we want to give the children more than just a roof over their heads. When I started here six years ago . . . let's just say, there was still room for improvement, but I'm proud to say we've since been rated as outstanding by the inspectors.'

'So I guess you'll stay on, in spite of your husband's death?' Lena asked casually.

'Of course. I owe him that much, and the children too. We've created a refuge here for tortured little souls. I would never forgive myself if I gave up now.'

Lena nodded. 'If we might get back to the afternoon in question. So, you're not entirely certain whether your husband was at home?'

Sabine Bohlen shrugged. 'No, I'm not.'

'And from four o'clock onwards? You said the children are busy with other things then.'

'I think he worked in his office and later had dinner with us. That's how it was every day. I then attended a parent–teacher evening at school. We take turns with those, or else they soon get too much.'

'And your husband stayed home?'

'I assume so, although he wasn't here when I got back.' Sabine Bohlen swallowed and blinked away her tears. 'I didn't think anything of it because he likes to go for walks in the evening.' She paused and again stared down at her hands. 'Liked.'

Lena signalled Johann not to ask any more questions for now. He stood up, took a glass from a cabinet and filled it with mineral water from a bottle on the table.

'Here you go,' he said, handing the glass to Frau Bohlen. She shot him another grateful look and drained the water in one go.

After a few moments, Lena continued, 'Your husband was found in a beach chair. Was he—?'

'We rent two beach chairs so we can take the kids down to the sea any time we want. My husband liked to sit there in the evenings.'

'I see,' Lena said. 'The death certificate issued by Dr Neumann states that your husband died of a heart attack and that he'd been suffering from a heart condition for a long time. Was he on any medication?'

Sabine Bohlen nodded.

Johann cleared his throat. 'Would you mind showing us his medication, Frau Bohlen?'

Sabine Bohlen hesitated briefly, then stood up and left the office. She returned a short while later with four boxes of pills, which she handed to Johann.

'Did your husband have acute symptoms?' asked Johann.

'No, not as far as I know. Dr Neumann examined him about every six months, unless something else came up in between, like a bad cold or back pain.'

'You demanded a post-mortem following your husband's death,' Lena said. 'Did you suspect that his death wasn't from natural causes?'

'*Suspect? Demanded?* You make it sound so bad! I'm not a detective and no doctor. I simply struggled to believe that all of a sudden . . . I merely voiced my doubts. What else could I do? And I didn't *insist* on the post-mortem, they just did it.'

Lena nodded. 'Did your husband have enemies?'

Sabine Bohlen scowled at Lena. 'Enemies? What an absurd thought! Ask anyone on this island and they will all give the same answer. My husband was kind, supportive and always there for other people. Someone like that doesn't have enemies – certainly no one who would wish him dead.'

'Well, unfortunately, it looks as though he did not die of natural causes,' Lena said as calmly as she could. 'And there is evidence that the perpetrator must have got very close to your husband.'

Sabine Bohlen stared at her. 'What do you mean exactly?'

'We can't discuss the details from the post-mortem for reasons pertaining to the investigation,' Johann said. 'I'm sure you understand,

Frau Bohlen. It's very important that you tell us about anything unusual you might have observed lately.'

Sabine Bohlen didn't look happy. *'Pertaining to the investigation?* What does that mean?' she asked. 'Are you trying to pin something on my husband?'

'Of course not, Frau Bohlen,' said Johann gently. 'It's simply that we're not permitted to repeat certain things during interview: rules and regulations, you know.'

Sabine Bohlen seemed somewhat appeased. She shrugged and looked out of the window.

'Do you know if your husband still owed anything on the house?' asked Lena.

'A mortgage, you mean? I'm not sure. I have an appointment with our accountant in two days.'

'How would you describe your marriage? Any problems?' Lena tried to sound casual.

Sabine Bohlen scowled at her again. 'What sort of question is that?'

'Purely routine, Frau Bohlen, so please answer the question,' Johann said in an attempt to mollify her.

'If I must. We were happy – don't forget, we didn't just share a house, we worked side by side every day.'

'So you never argued at all?' asked Lena.

'I really don't understand how that's any of your business. We loved each other. Isn't that enough?'

'I'm sorry, Frau Bohlen, but everything becomes our business in the course of an investigation like this,' Lena said. 'Did you notice anything out of the ordinary about your husband's behaviour in the days or weeks preceding his death? Was he particularly nervous, agitated or irritable, perhaps?'

'Out of the ordinary? Our work with the children here can be exhausting. My husband had been doing this job for many years, and it's only natural that things get a little heated from time to time. He may have been a little more highly strung than usual. One of our boys has been a headache, and my husband was worried about him. But other than that – no, nothing out of the ordinary.'

'If I follow correctly, you only saw your husband very briefly that day. How did he seem?'

'The same as always. Maybe a little absent-minded – yes, I think he was. We went for a walk along the mudflats the day before, and normally we'd talk about the children – there's always something to discuss – but that day, he was quiet, deep in thought.'

'I understand. Now, we need to know where you were on the evening of your husband's death.'

Sabine Bohlen stared at Lena aghast. Then she snarled, 'Here. Where else?'

'Can anyone verify that?' asked Lena.

'I don't know. We have a separate flat within the house. I may have gone back to the office or checked on the children at some point.'

'You don't know for sure?'

'No, I already told you.'

'Were you asleep when Sergeant Reimers called you?'

'I was on my way to bed.'

Johann cleared his throat. 'Do you remember what time that was, Frau Bohlen?' He smiled at her.

'I usually go to bed at around eleven. It was a little later that night, around twenty past to half past eleven.' Sabine Bohlen got to her feet. 'Look, I'm sorry, but I really must get back to work now before our entire routine's mucked up for the day.'

Lena rose slowly. 'We also need to interview the rest of the staff. Can we start with your teacher, Frau Müller?'

'No, Isabel won't be here for at least another couple of hours,' Sabine Bohlen said coolly. 'She's gone shopping with our cook. But the cleaner is here.'

The police are on the island. CID. They don't believe he died of a heart attack: murder or suicide. As if it mattered. He's dead, that's all that matters.

That dumb island copper thought he was so clever. Natural causes, he said. And the doctor believed it too.

But now those detectives are here to stir everything up. They'll have to ask the right questions to get the right answers.

But this whole country's corrupt – why should the police be any different? They're part of the system and have to function, carry out orders, serve, just like everyone else.

He's dead. He deserves to be dead. Dead as a bloody doornail. It's the only right and fitting punishment for an evil person.

There are far too many evil people like him. They're everywhere – in the police force, the tax office, the council – anyone could be one of them.

I won't ever fail again.

I promised.

5

'So?' asked Lena once Johann had climbed into the car. 'What do you think about our little talk with Frau Bohlen?'

They'd spent the last ten minutes interviewing the cleaner. She'd only worked at the home for two months, and she'd had the day off when Hein Bohlen died. Lena knew after a few questions that this woman had nothing to contribute to the case.

'Hard to say,' Johann replied. 'I'm struggling to read Sabine Bohlen. At times I felt like she had no interest in seeing her husband's death explained, but then a few moments later she'd be all cooperative again.'

'Yes, I agree – some conflict of feelings there. I also got the impression that she knows more than she's letting on. She could be trying to protect her husband's reputation, or that of the home – or herself?'

Johann pulled the list Sabine Bohlen had given him from his briefcase. It held around a dozen names.

'A nice move to ask for the list in advance,' Lena said, 'and you're also very good at playing the "good cop". We'll make the most of that.' Johann didn't reply. 'That was a compliment, by the way. I must admit I underestimated you a tiny bit. Like I said, I think we're on the road to becoming a good team.'

Johann ran his hand through his hair. 'Thanks!'

'You're welcome.' Lena nodded in approval. 'OK, let's talk about Frau Bohlen later and head off to see Dr Neumann in Wittdün.'

'He'll claim doctor–patient confidentiality.'

'Of course he will, but we still have to interview him.' She started up the engine. 'Call and let him know we're coming, will you?'

After driving across the island, they pulled up outside a newish building in the centre of Wittdün. Hein Bohlen's GP, tall and good-looking with blond hair, emerged from his office shortly after their arrival. He shook Lena's hand and introduced himself.

'I'm Detective Inspector Lena Lorenzen, CID Kiel, and this is DS Grasmann from Flensburg.'

'Oh, representatives from right across Schleswig-Holstein. Shall we talk in my office?'

Once they were all seated, Dr Neumann looked at them expectantly. 'I'm guessing this is about one of my patients, Hein Bohlen?'

Lena nodded. 'That's correct. You—'

'I'd like to point out right away that I'm bound by doctor–patient confidentiality, but you'll be aware of that already.'

'Of course. We only have a few questions. You noted on the death certificate that Hein Bohlen died of a heart attack and that there was a relevant previous condition.'

'That's right.'

'You had no doubts over the cause of his death?'

'No, none at all. As his doctor, I was familiar with his medical history and had no doubts whatsoever.'

Lena placed the four boxes of medication on the table. 'Frau Bohlen gave us these. Can you please tell us what they are?'

'Simply put, they're all drugs to prevent a heart attack.' He picked up one of the boxes. 'This one's the most important: it's an anti-platelet drug, which means it inhibits the blood's ability to clot and therefore reduces the danger of vascular obstruction. I always prescribe them in such cases.' He opened the box, took out the half-empty blister pack and studied it. 'Yes, they're the right ones.'

He pointed to the next box. 'Beta blockers and ACE inhibitors, both of which treat high blood pressure, and then, lastly, this one: a drug to control high cholesterol levels.' He pushed the four boxes back over to Lena.

'Is it unusual for someone to take this medication and have a heart attack anyway?' asked Lena.

'Well, they're merely preventative. If the patient isn't too far gone already, they should work pretty well, although there are other factors that can lead to a heart attack.'

'Such as stress? Excitement?'

'That's possible.'

'What happens if a patient fails to take the medication regularly, or not at all?'

'Russian roulette, I'd say, with more than one bullet in the cylinder. But a good doctor can spot when a patient doesn't take their medication regularly. I haven't had it happen in all my years as a GP.'

'So you can't imagine that anyone would commit suicide that way?'

'No, I can't. It would take far too long, and then what? The patient would try and wind himself up on purpose to raise his blood pressure? No, I really can't imagine anyone doing that.'

Lena nodded. 'What if the patient was diagnosed with another, worse disease, such as terminal cancer? Mightn't he consider ending it then?'

'Perhaps, but this is getting very far-fetched, don't you think?'

Johann had followed the conversation with growing interest and seemed to be holding back some questions of his own.

'If you say so,' Lena said. 'Now, I'd like to ask a few things about the night in question.'

Dr Neumann smiled. 'Go ahead.'

'You received the call just after eleven, is that right?'

Dr Neumann frowned in consternation. 'No, let me think . . . It must have been later. About twenty past, I'd say?'

'Are you absolutely sure?' asked Lena.

Dr Neumann crossed the room to pull a folder from a shelf and inspect its contents. 'Here we go: five to twelve. That's the time on the death certificate. If I count back from that . . . No, it must have been later – at least twenty past.' He placed the folder back on the shelf and returned to his seat.

'Who was at the scene?' asked Lena.

'Walter Reimers. He was the one who called me. Apparently, the couple who found Hein Bohlen left just before I got there. I never met them so I can't tell you anything about them.'

'How long did it take you to get to the beach?'

'I was on call that night. About quarter of an hour, I'd say, perhaps a little less.'

'How long had Herr Bohlen been dead by then?'

'I'm not a pathologist, but from my experience I'd say at least an hour.'

'How long were you at the beach?'

'My examination only took a few minutes, then we waited for the hearse. I can't tell you precisely, but no more than half an hour, maybe even less.' Dr Neumann looked a little confused. 'I don't understand why you're asking me all this. Walter Reimers can tell you much more than me and he'll have it all noted down in his report.'

'Just routine inquiries,' Johann said, speaking for the first time. 'What was your impression when you got to the beach? How was Hein Bohlen positioned? Was there anything to indicate that he wasn't alone when he died?'

'The questions you're asking! I'm a doctor, not a detective, and I wasn't on the lookout for anything like that. Like I said, ask your colleague. Is there anything else I can do for you? My patients are waiting.'

'One last thing,' Lena said, pulling a blister pack from one of the boxes of medication. 'You said this was the most important drug. Would it be conceivable for someone to swap the tablets?'

Dr Neumann took the blister pack from her. 'See here: the name of the medicine and the manufacturer are printed on the push-through packaging. If you try to remove the foil, it tears. Basically, you'd have to produce a whole new sheet of pills, and you'd struggle with that unless you happened to be the owner of a pharmaceutical company. In other words, it would be near impossible for ordinary mortals such as ourselves.' He slid the pills back into the box and handed it over to Lena. 'And like I said earlier, it would be extremely tedious and unpredictable – not an ideal way to kill someone.'

Dr Neumann stood up and the two investigators followed him to the door.

'You've been very helpful,' Lena said, shaking his hand. 'We know where to find you if we have any more questions.'

Johann Grasmann leaned back in the passenger seat. 'Quite a nuisance, that doctor–patient confidentiality. Wouldn't it be in the patient's best interests to reveal all?'

'I thought our island doctor was quite informative, actually. Any news from Hanover yet?'

Johann checked his emails on his phone. 'Yep, a few minutes ago.' He read the message and passed his phone over to Lena.

'Well, would you look at that!' Lena murmured. 'We'd better pay Sergeant Reimers another visit. Can you call ahead, please?'

Ten minutes later, they pulled up outside Amrum police station. Lena got out of the car and waited for Johann, who was on the phone to his colleague in Hanover, checking that they'd understood the email correctly. He gave her a brief nod as he joined her. Just then, the door opened and they were greeted by Reimers, the same studied smile on his face as before.

'Have you settled in all right?' he asked once they'd all taken a seat in his office. 'I heard you've been speaking with Sabine.'

'And we're fresh from interviewing Dr Neumann,' Lena said.

'Part and parcel, I guess,' Reimers replied. 'So where do you go from here?'

'We're slowly working our way through the list of interviews,' Johann said, his face serious. 'Dr Neumann couldn't tell us much about the night of Hein Bohlen's death. He wasn't at the beach for long.'

'That's right.'

'In your report, it says you arrived at the scene at eleven p.m. Is that correct?' Johann's question sounded casual – a necessary formality.

'That's correct. I wouldn't have written it in the report otherwise.'

Lena listened with interest. She had to admit that her first impression of Johann Grasmann hadn't been that favourable, but here he was, impressing her with his skill all over again.

'The two witnesses who found Hein Bohlen left the scene shortly after eleven, right?'

Reimers rose abruptly. 'What are you playing at, Sergeant?'

Johann wasn't rattled. He turned one page after the other in his little notebook until he seemed to have found what he was looking for. Reimers was still on his feet.

'Standard inquiries. You know the score. We're just trying to get a clear picture.' He turned another page. 'Yup, there it is. Both witnesses stated that they left the beach shortly after your arrival. Is that correct?'

Reimers sat back down slowly. 'I checked on Herr Bohlen to make there was no pulse, then I questioned the witnesses briefly and sent them home. They were in shock. Why should they have stayed?'

Lena suppressed a smile when her Flensburg colleague started leafing through his little book again.

'I'm just struggling with the timeline here. Dr Neumann told us you called him at twenty past eleven at the earliest. That would be—'

'He must be mistaken. I called him as soon as the witnesses had left.' Reimers was growing increasingly agitated.

Johann pulled a manila folder from his briefcase and took out a sheet of paper. 'Yes, I remembered correctly. The time on the death certificate reads five to midnight.'

Reimers grabbed the document and studied it. 'His watch must have been wrong. I admit I forgot to check his entries. Jesus – the man died of natural causes, his GP confirmed it, and you're making a fuss about a typo!'

Lena cleared her throat. 'I agree, we're not here to split hairs. I'm sure the funeral home will confirm your timing, if we have to double-check at all. We're much more interested in finding out if there was anyone who disliked Hein Bohlen, or even hated him?'

Reimers seemed reassured by the change of subject. He leaned back in his chair. 'Ever since I was told that foul play can't be ruled out, I've been asking myself the same question. Hein – Herr Bohlen, I mean – was well liked around here. I can't imagine that he had any enemies, let alone anyone who would want him dead. We're on Amrum, not in Hamburg or Berlin.'

'You knew him well?' asked Lena.

'I can't say we were friends, but we knew each other well enough and had a beer every once in a while. That's just the way it is on Amrum. I first came here eight years ago and met Hein Bohlen when one of his charges ran away – thankfully, we caught the boy on the ferry.'

'The evidence we have so far suggests that Hein Bohlen was indeed murdered,' Lena said, changing direction again. 'Since there's nothing to suggest that Herr Bohlen was the victim of a robbery, we're assuming that he knew the perpetrator.'

Sergeant Reimers nodded thoughtfully. 'I see what you mean. But, for the life of me, I can't think of anyone. I'll keep an ear open, of course. No problem at all.'

Lena rose, saying, 'Right then, we'd better get back to work.'

Johann stood up also and asked Reimers, 'I don't suppose you have the number of the funeral home to hand, do you?'

Reimers reached for a notepad, scribbled down a name and number and tore the sheet off before handing it to Johann with a forced smile. 'Here you go, Sergeant.'

6

'Strange conversation,' Johann said, back in the car. 'Why didn't we push him harder?'

'What use would that have been in this situation?'

'He might have lost his nerve. Something's definitely wrong here.'

'Maybe. But Sergeant Reimers is a police officer, not some petty criminal. Unless we have something concrete, a confrontation could backfire on us big time.'

'Still, I don't understand what he was doing for around twenty minutes before calling the doctor.'

'Don't worry, we'll get to the bottom of it – but I'd rather have a few trump cards up my sleeve before that.' Lena grinned. 'Makes a game of poker so much more fun.' She checked the time. 'Hungry?'

Johann shrugged. 'A little. Any decent takeaways around here?'

Lena started up the engine. 'Fast food is not my style, young man. Let me surprise you.'

They drove out of Nebel and headed south along the shoreline. A short while later, they reached a brick building painted white with green lattice windows. The restaurant stood not far from the Wadden Sea shoreline.

'Likedeeler,' said Johann, reading the sign. 'Weren't those—?'

'A guild of buccaneers, also known as the Victual Brothers. But don't you worry, you'll be quite safe.' Once inside the restaurant, they chose a table in a bay window overlooking the coast. Lena handed Johann a menu. 'The plaice with prawns always used to be good. The prawns at least come from the last remaining fisherman on Amrum.'

Once they'd ordered, Johann pulled his notebook from his pocket. 'Who are we going to interview next?' He unfolded Sabine Bohlen's list of names.

'The teacher at the home is expecting us at two. I'm hoping she'll give us a bit more than Frau Bohlen – we'll see. What have we got so far? The victim's wife told us very little about the day Hein Bohlen died, only that he hadn't been quite himself lately: irritable and distracted. We need to check if he really went to the supermarket that day and how long for. Can you take care of that?' Johann nodded. 'Good,' Lena said, then went on, 'Visiting the accountant strikes me as an important lead. Let's drive to Wittdün after the interview with Frau Müller. Can you call ahead?'

Johann made a note. 'Shouldn't we ask Frau Bohlen to relieve him of his pledge of confidentiality?'

'No, I want to let sleeping dogs lie on that one. I have a feeling she'd refuse and tell the man to keep his mouth shut. She seems awfully worried about her husband's good name, and that of the home as well. Let's just give it a try.' She cleared her throat. 'All right, what do we have? A wife who is passionate about her work and on the surface seemed relatively composed when we talked to her. The educational side of the business appears more important to her than the finances, considering it's now over two weeks since her husband's death and she still hasn't seen her accountant. She is, after all, the sole beneficiary. She wasn't too fussed about what her husband was up to all day long, and he was often out at night too. Long walks, she says. Doesn't sound like the happiest of marriages to me. We'll see.

'The GP was very happy to help in spite of doctor–patient confidentiality. His opinion sounds plausible. I'll double-check the medical facts with our pathologists. If we find any irregularities, we'll have to pay him another visit, but if he insists on his pledge of confidentiality, there's nothing we can do about it – unless he uses it to cover up a crime, although we have nothing to suggest that's the case. And then we have our colleague Reimers. He's—'

'Oh, yes,' Johann said with fervour. 'Can we get our hands on his personnel file?'

'I don't think so – you know how tough the regs are. Obviously, I'll have a go anyway. We don't have anything apart from a time discrepancy, which Reimers blames on human error. We need to take a look at his previous placements in the force – see if there's anything of interest.'

'Got it. We need to keep an open mind. You're absolutely right, but I just – how can I put it? – I can't stand police who don't stick to the rules.'

Lena looked thoughtful. 'I don't always stick to the rules.'

Johann gave a start. 'I didn't mean it like that. Sometimes unconventional methods of investigation are necessary.'

Lena grinned. 'That sounds more like it.' Then she turned serious again. 'I absolutely detest a bent copper too – not that I'm suggesting for a moment that Walter Reimers is in that category. If we find anything else that doesn't feel right, we'll find out what's going on.'

'OK, I'm in!' Johann said enthusiastically.

'But softly, softly, please. We don't want to shoot ourselves in the foot.'

A waiter brought their lunch. Johann had ordered a prawn salad and Lena the plaice. She used to come here regularly with her mother and Beke. The three of them would walk along the coastal path from Nebel and back again after their meal. She remembered their long conversations. She'd learned a lot about Amrum and life on the island during those walks. Her family had lived here for generations; her great-grandfather had been a captain of whaling ships and her Aunt Beke still lived in the house he'd built on his retirement.

'The case?' asked Johann when he noticed Lena's faraway expression.

'Old memories,' Lena replied. 'How do you like the far north so far?'

Johann looked surprised. 'Me? Well enough, I guess. The North Frisians can seem a little stand-offish, but . . .' He faltered. 'Not all. Present company excluded, of course.'

Lena smirked, ate the last morsel of fish and then pushed her plate aside. 'Stand-offish? That's interesting. What about people on the Lower Rhine then? Are they any more approachable?'

'No, not really – more like stubborn and suspicious of strangers.' He grinned. 'Except during carnival season, of course. There's none of that "them and us" nonsense then – everyone's suddenly your brother or sister.'

'Better once a year than never,' Lena said seriously.

Johann seemed to ponder Lena's comment. Eventually, he said, 'Well, I'm not sure. Carnival isn't really my thing. Dressing up, getting drunk, being cheerful – all at the push of a button?'

'If it makes people happy, why not?'

Johann stood up. 'Are you ready to go? I'll get the bill.'

He turned away without waiting for Lena's reply and walked over to the waiter. She watched her colleague as he pulled out his wallet and placed several banknotes on the bar. Once the waiter had given him a receipt, Lena rose and walked to the door.

◆ ◆ ◆

A young woman in her mid-twenties sat facing the two detectives. Of medium height, she was slim and wore jeans and a tight-fitting sweat-shirt. Her shoulder-length brown hair was tied in a loose ponytail.

'How long have you been working at the home?' Lena asked after checking Isabel Müller's ID.

'Six months and three weeks, almost to the day,' the young woman replied.

They were sitting in the office of the home. Sabine Bohlen had left them a few minutes earlier.

'Why choose Amrum?'

'Coincidence. I was out of a job and heard about the position. I called, came for an interview the next day and started a week later.'

'Do you live here at the home?'

'Yes, it's easier that way. It's nearly impossible to find a flat that's affordable on the island.'

'Have you always worked in this field?'

'In the broader sense of the word, yes: I've worked with children and young people. But I only finished my degree three years ago.'

Johann Grasmann cleared his throat. 'Did you know your predecessor?' He checked his notebook. 'Anna Bauer. She worked here for five years.'

'No, only from what the children told me, and Frau Bohlen dropped a comment here and there.'

'How was your relationship with Hein Bohlen?' asked Lena.

'He was my employer. How do you describe a relationship with your employer? Normal, professional. We got along fine.'

'Did you like him?'

'As a person, you mean?'

'For example.'

'Well, he was from a different generation. Twice my age. I appreciated his experience with children and teenagers. I learned a lot from him.'

'And on a personal level?'

'How do you mean? We weren't friends or anything. He was my boss and I tried to keep a professional distance.'

'Did he share your views?'

'I have no idea what you're getting at.' Irritated, Isabel Müller brushed a strand of hair out of her face. 'I had nothing to do with Herr Bohlen outside of work. We only interacted on a professional basis, though of course you still get to know someone reasonably well that way. You could say he was . . . Don't get me wrong, he was very polite most of the time, but when he was in a bad mood, everyone knew about it.'

'Hein Bohlen had a bit of a temper?'

'No, I didn't say that – he had his quirks, you could say. A little hot-tempered from time to time, but never towards the children. He was always very professional with the children. But you asked about my opinion of him as a person.'

'Hot-tempered, moody and very polite,' said Lena in summary. 'Let's leave it at that for now.' She smiled at Isabel Müller and asked abruptly, 'Where were you on the evening of Herr Bohlen's death?'

'Me?' asked Isabel Müller with amusement. 'Am I a suspect?'

'We have to ask everyone. Where were you between nine and eleven p.m.?'

'Well, here. I was on night duty, so I could hardly leave. We take it in turns, Herr and Frau Bohlen and me.' She paused. 'Used to take turns.'

'Can Frau Bohlen confirm that? Or one of the older children?'

Isabel Müller thought for a moment. 'Frau Bohlen was in her flat. We don't usually cross paths during the evening. And the children? It's not like a hospital, where patients are nursed round the clock. The children don't often call out after bedtime. No, there wasn't anything that evening. We only have one fourteen-year-old at the moment. The others are younger: twelve, eleven, ten, down to seven. They're asleep at that time of night.'

Lena nodded. 'And you're absolutely certain you didn't notice anything out of the ordinary that evening? Everything was the same as usual?'

'I only found out about the death the next morning. I'm sure I'd remember if anything happened that night. No, everything was exactly the same.'

Johann wrote something in his trusty notebook. 'Did you notice anything odd about Hein Bohlen's behaviour? On the day he died or the days before?'

'No, not that I can think of.'

'Take your time. It may have been small changes you wouldn't usually pay attention to. Was he more on edge than usual, did his routine change during his last few days, was he at home more than normal, or perhaps less?'

'I honestly can't say for sure. One day merges into the next here. I'm worried I'm imagining it, but – his fuse may have been a little shorter than usual, perhaps he was a little more distracted. But, like I said, it might just . . .' She broke off in the middle of the sentence and smiled.

'What exactly do you base that observation on?' asked Lena. 'Can you give us an example?'

Isabel Müller sighed. 'That's where it gets tricky, hence my fear that I'm imagining things, but all right. We work with children of various ages. Almost all of them come from dysfunctional families and have had a ton of bad experiences in their short lives. If either of you grew up with siblings, you know how turbulent life can be in a family of only two or three children – and that's in a perfectly normal family. What I'm trying to say is, you need nerves of steel in this job from morning till night. If you're not in complete control of yourself when you work with children, they soon notice and withdraw or take advantage. I'm not saying we have to be like machines, but whenever we're around our children here, we need to be very aware of our own state of mind. To get to the point, even weeks before he' – she paused to search for the right words – 'before his death, Herr Bohlen could be quite impatient with the kids. One time I saw him nearly hit Jonas. Like I said – nearly. Jonas is one of our children who needs a lot of attention and demands it very actively. He's ten and going through a difficult phase. Herr Bohlen immediately pulled himself together, but I don't know what would have happened if I hadn't walked into the room right then.'

'And was that just one of many similar incidents?' asked Lena.

'It was just an example – a very drastic example – and I'd like to ask you not to tell Frau Bohlen. I don't know how she'd react right now.'

'Let's forget about Frau Bohlen for the moment and stay with your boss. He'd had a rather short fuse in recent weeks. That's what you said, wasn't it?'

'Yes, that's what I said.' Isabel Müller leaned forward and rested her elbows on the table, then changed her mind and straightened up again. She hadn't leaned back against her chair once during the entire interview. 'Yes, there were other similar situations. Each taken on their own, they wouldn't have seemed significant. We're only human, and that's good.'

'Do you have any idea why Herr Bohlen's behaviour might have been a little out of the ordinary?'

Isabel Müller shrugged. 'How should I know?'

'You may have noticed something,' said Johann. 'Any small detail could be significant. Was there trouble with any of the staff or trouble at home? Was the phone ringing more than usual in the previous few days?'

'If I'd known what was going to happen, I'd have paid more attention. But now, more than two weeks later, I really can't say. I never really hear the phone calls because I rarely work in the office. And I don't know of any trouble in the house. And with his wife . . . Well, what marriage is perfect? But you're better off asking Frau Bohlen about that. I'd rather not comment.' She paused. 'Hang on, I think a few days before he died we did have some visitors I didn't recognise. I was on my way to pick the kids up from school. A car pulled up just as I was about to get into the minibus. Two men got out. I remember they were wearing dark suits, and in their forties or fifties, I'd say. But I only saw them out of the corner of my eye, and by the time I got back they were gone.'

'Was Frau Bohlen at home?' asked Johann.

Isabel Müller thought for a moment. 'No, I'm pretty sure she was on the mainland that day, visiting a friend in Hamburg. At least I think it was that day . . .'

'How long before Bohlen's death was this?'

'Four or five days – a week, tops.'

Johann scribbled something in his little book.

'Was there anyone else in the house? The cook, perhaps?'

'No idea. I really can't remember.'

'Do you remember any details of the number plate?' asked Lena.

'Hamburg – yes, I'm pretty sure the licence plate started with HH.'

'Make? Colour?'

'Some kind of big, dark limo. I'm not much into cars. BMW or Mercedes? They all look the same to me.'

'Was Herr Bohlen different from usual when you got back to the home that afternoon?'

Isabel Müller nodded. 'Yes. Remember the incident I told you about?'

'With Jonas?' asked Lena.

'Yes. It happened that afternoon.'

It's high time I did something. I made a promise – to myself and to him.

Am I too weak? Was my first step the last? No! I waited much too long, kept putting it off until it was too late. I won't make that mistake again. It will all have been for nothing if I give up now.

That man deserved to die. That's what I told myself a thousand times, and I was right a thousand times.

No, I'm not sorry for him.

But I killed someone.

I imagine him sitting in that beach chair, gasping for breath. He can't understand what's happening to him, but there's mortal fear in his eyes. He screams without making a sound. He's begging me to help him. But I just stand there and watch from a safe distance.

Every night I watch him in my dreams. Over and over.

But he deserved to die. If I don't carry on now, it was all for nothing. No one would ever learn the truth. Everything would be forgotten. Everything! The pain, the screams, the tears, the awful, never-ending nightmares.

I made a solemn promise.

I have to see this through to the end.

Or I'll never sleep again.

7

Back in the car, Johann jotted something down in his book and then put it aside. 'Shame the cook has the day off. We could have got her interview over and done with.'

Lena started the car. 'Actually, I prefer having a little time to digest the details of each interview. Sometimes parts of a conversation can take on an entirely new meaning over time. We'll question her in the morning.'

She drove back on to the main road, passed through Norddorf, and continued south.

'Let's pay the accountant a visit and then swing by the funeral home. With a bit of luck, someone will be in.'

'OK,' Johann said. 'By the way, the accountant wasn't very cooperative over the phone. He didn't want to speak to us at all until I threatened to interview him down at the station in Husum, although he still insisted that he's bound by his pledge of confidentiality.'

'Interesting. One confidentiality clause a day is usually enough for me. We could apply for a court order, but God knows how long that would take – and then the great trawl through the books would begin. I suggest we take a hard line with this one.' She sighed.

Johann nodded. 'Will we be interviewing anyone else today?'

'Once we've done the accountant and the funeral director, you mean? Not at this stage. But you could try to get a bit of background on Isabel Müller. Just the usual to begin with: where she grew up, parents, siblings, university. See what you can find out. And the same for Sabine Bohlen, please. And before I forget, add Anna Bauer to the list, Frau Müller's predecessor. I'd really like to know why she quit her job so suddenly.'

'OK, that should keep me busy for a while.'

'I know, but we have nothing solid so far. And I can't shake the feeling that there's more to this than murder or manslaughter – or whatever it was.'

'Do you want me to run a background check on Sergeant Reimers too?'

'No, I'll take care of that.' Lena glanced at Johann. 'One more thing. Not one word gets out to anyone without my knowledge. Not to anyone! Not to your colleagues in Flensburg, and not to your boss.'

Johann swallowed. 'I wasn't going to.'

'Don't get me wrong. I trust you, but I know how easily something can slip out, especially with workmates. And if your boss wants to know anything, tell him I told you to keep your mouth shut. He can contact me.'

'O–K,' Johann said, drawing out the syllables.

Meanwhile, they had arrived in Nebel. Lena slowed the car and pointed over to a whitewashed building identified as a church by its bell tower. The building had a thatched roof and stood in the middle of a cemetery.

'That's where I was christened. If we get time in the next few days, I'll show you the talking gravestones. A big tourist attraction.'

'Sounds pretty high-tech.'

Lena laughed. 'Quite the opposite. You'll be amazed. And I'll drag you up to the lighthouse too. It's one of the few around the North Sea that tourists are allowed to go up. The view from the top is stunning.' Johann didn't say anything. 'Only if it brings us nearer to the truth, of course. Who knows, we may yet have to question the pastor. Sadly, there hasn't been a lighthouse keeper for a long time.'

'Why are we checking up on Isabel Müller?' asked Johann abruptly. 'D'you sense anything suspicious about her? Absolutely nothing about her rang any alarm bells for me.'

'Just a feeling. And since we have no firm clues of any type yet, we may as well be thorough.'

'A feeling? That wouldn't be enough for me to go on.'

'I just thought she was a little too eager. I might be completely wrong, but a healthy dose of scepticism comes with the job. We have to speculate, double-check and dig around in the past. It's the only way we can rule people out. I hate surprises when there's something I should have figured out sooner.'

'I understand,' Johann said unconvincingly.

They passed the first houses of Wittdün. Lena turned off the main road and parked outside a plain, two-storey brick building. They climbed out of the car and walked to the front door.

'If Mr Accountant sticks to his pledge of confidentiality, we'll apply a little pressure,' Lena said. 'The usual game.' Johann nodded hesitantly. 'You'll be fine,' she said with a smile. 'Why don't you play "bad cop" this time?'

'But—' Johann said, but Lena raised her hand.

'You'll be fine. Improvise. If I ask you to fetch something from the car, leave us for a while. Or just go anyway, if you reckon he'll only talk to me.'

'OK then,' said Johann and rang the bell.

'Tamme Lüschen,' said the man in the beige suit, shaking Lena's hand. He was of average height, around forty, with slicked-back hair. His smile looked studied. 'So you're here about Hein Bohlen.'

Lena introduced herself and Johann. The accountant had met them in the reception area of his office and showed no intention of asking them in any further. 'Is there anywhere we can talk in private?' she asked.

'Certainly.' Tamme Lüschen stepped aside. 'My office. It's the first door on the right.'

Once all three were seated, Tamme Lüschen asked if they'd like anything to drink.

'No, thanks,' Lena replied. 'You were Hein Bohlen's accountant?'

'Yes, that's correct. When the home opened . . .' Tamme Lüschen paused to think. 'Must be about fourteen years now. I've offered him my services ever since.'

'Were you and Herr Bohlen friends?'

Tamme Lüschen leaned back in his chair. 'We were business partners and well acquainted. I wouldn't go so far as to say we were friends.'

'How often did you see him?'

'Well, once a year here in the office to discuss the year-end accounts, and every now and then in between if something came up.'

'Meaning?'

'Homes get audited too. When their audit was due, we'd meet up to discuss the details before and after.'

'We still have a few gaps in Hein Bohlen's last day. His wife thought he might have had an appointment with you. Is that right?'

'No, we had no appointment. I didn't see him that day.'

'When was the home last audited?' asked Lena.

'I'm pledged to confidentiality. I neither want to nor am permitted to say anything on the subject.'

'Do you have the results?'

Tamme Lüschen leaned forward and smiled. 'Have I not made myself perfectly clear? You know very well that I can't give out any information without the client's express permission. I assume Frau Bohlen hasn't granted it, and I would strongly advise her not to do so. I think we've finished here.'

Lena ignored his last comment and smiled back at him. 'That's a pity.'

Johann cleared his throat. 'Herr Lüschen, we've heard rumours that the home is in dire straits financially.'

Tamme Lüschen pretended to be shocked. 'Is that right? It's amazing what people gossip about. And where did you hear this rumour, may I ask?'

'We can always apply for an official court order, if you'd prefer,' Johann said, 'and then it's just a matter of time. And you know what that means, don't you?'

'What do you mean?' The accountant looked a little less sure of himself.

'A court order covers access to all files in your office. In other words, several police officers will sift through all your documents for hours. I'm guessing you'd rather avoid that kind of PR?'

Tamme Lüschen looked from one detective to the other. 'You're not serious?'

Lena Lorenzen straightened up a little. 'I was hoping we might find a way to avoid that particular scenario.'

'An accountant's pledge of confidentiality is a serious business. I just can't see any leeway.'

'I didn't want to have to tell you this,' Johann said. 'But according to the rumours, you helped Hein Bohlen doctor the books. I'm talking about more than mere tax evasion.'

'How dare you?' exclaimed Tamme Lüschen. 'That's outrageous!'

Johann shrugged innocently. 'We rely on tip-offs from concerned citizens. The accusations sounded plausible to us. Like I said, we've heard the rumours and we need to check them out. I had hoped you'd prove more cooperative and we could get this all sorted here and now.' He rose. 'Never mind. Please excuse me for a moment. I'm expecting a call from the chief prosecutor.' He gave Tamme Lüschen a curt nod and left the office without waiting for a reply.

'What just happened?' said Tamme Lüschen, more to himself than to Lena.

'Oh, my young colleague can be a little gung-ho. If it were up to him, he'd bring a special unit along to every single assignment. But his success rate speaks for itself and state prosecutors do love a case to be solved.'

'Special unit?' Tamme Lüschen seemed utterly confused.

'You know, the ones with guns and vests and helmets. Young people these days, eh? Herr Lüschen, don't you think we can look for a compromise? I understand completely that you're bound by your pledge, but you must understand our position too. We have a duty to find out the truth.'

'Compromise? What are you suggesting?' Tamme Lüschen asked hesitantly.

'Easy. You answer a few questions – off the record – and I promise that no one will ever learn about it. If I decide that a court order is necessary after all, however, you'd have to hand over the information officially.' Tamme Lüschen glanced at the door. 'My colleague's sitting in the car and will be speaking with the prosecutor any minute. Or I can send him a text saying that we no longer need the order. It's your call!'

The accountant groaned. 'What do you want to know?'

Lena nodded and texted Johann to wait in the car. Then she looked up and asked, 'When was the audit?'

'About six weeks ago.'

'Do you have the results?'

'No, not yet. For some reason, the tax office is taking its time.'

'Are there irregularities?'

Tamme Lüschen hesitated. 'That's a matter of interpretation. I don't know if they'll come back with anything – but even then, it's not usually a problem. They name a sum for back payments and the issue is sorted.'

'What's the home's financial situation?'

'Not too bad. The house is paid off and the home almost always operates at capacity.'

'But?'

Tamme Lüschen took his time. Eventually, he said, 'There have been several large personal withdrawals lately.'

'Cash withdrawals?' The accountant nodded. 'How large?'

'Around eighty thousand euros in total, over a period of about six months.'

'The business account is in the red?'

'You could say that.'

'What has the bank got to say about that?'

'You'd need to ask them.'

'Herr Lüschen! I thought we were aiming for a compromise?' Lena cleared her throat. 'I'm guessing the bank hit the brakes?'

'In a manner of speaking.'

'Was the audit conducted because of the cash withdrawals? Had someone tipped off the tax office?'

Tamme Lüschen didn't reply.

'I understand,' said Lena. 'OK, another question: the house Herr Bohlen bought for the home must have cost at least a million. Am I right?'

'Including renovations and fittings, you'd need to add half as much again.'

'You said the house was paid off. How big was the loan?'

'Not very big.'

'Herr Lüschen, do I have to drag everything out of you? As soon as I've got what I want, you're rid of me. So?'

'A hundred and fifty thousand.'

'Wow! And where did the rest come from?'

Tamme Lüschen shook his head. 'I honestly don't know.' When Lena still didn't respond, he said, 'You have to believe me! I never asked. I only became his accountant once the home opened.'

'One last question: where were you on the night Herr Bohlen was found dead? Between nine and eleven p.m. in particular?'

Tamme Lüschen stared at her in shock. 'Why are you asking me? I had nothing whatsoever to do with Hein Bohlen's death.'

'Where were you?'

'At home. Like I am almost every night.'

'Can anyone verify that?'

'My wife, of course. Feel free to ask her.' Tamme Lüschen scribbled a number on a piece of paper and handed it to Lena. 'That's my home number so you can get hold of her.'

Lena pulled a card with her own details from her bag and placed it on the table in front of the accountant. 'Just in case you think of anything else. Our arrangement still stands. Better you come to us instead of us coming across your name again during the investigation.'

Tamme Lüschen stared at the card, an unhappy look on his face. 'Can you find your own way out?'

'I think so,' said Lena. 'Break the news gently to Sabine Bohlen. Her nerves aren't the best at the moment.' She left the office without waiting for a reply.

'So, did it work?' asked Johann as soon as Lena got in the car.

Lena grinned. 'Bang your fist on the table next time – literally – and we'll truly be the dream team.' She told Johann briefly what she'd learned.

'Interesting,' he said. 'Gambling or blackmail?'

'We'll have to find out. Can you take care of the tax office tomorrow and let them know we're after some intel? I'll try to get a court order. They must have the source of the money in their records. Hein Bohlen can't previously have earned that much as a social educator and manager of a children's home.'

'Inherited, perhaps? Or a private loan?'

'We'll see.' Lena started the car. 'Off to the realm of the dead we go.'

8

The funeral home lay on a quiet side street. A large showroom had been tacked on to a small townhouse. They went in by the main entrance and were met by a serious-looking man in his mid-fifties wearing a black suit. His balding head gleamed. He looked back and forth between the two detectives.

'Lars Meiners,' he said. 'How can I help?'

'Detective Inspector Lorenzen,' Lena said and held up her police pass. 'This is DS Johann Grasmann.'

'Lorenzen? Are you the daughter of—?'

'This is not a social call, Herr Meiners. We're investigating the death of Hein Bohlen. Is there anywhere we can talk?'

The man nodded and led them through to his office. 'So how can I be of assistance?' he asked, once he'd closed the door.

'You collected Hein Bohlen's body from the beach, is that correct?' asked Lena.

'Yes, that was me. It's my job.'

'Who called you?'

Lars Meiners looked at them in surprise. 'You don't know that? It was your colleague from the island, Walter Reimers.'

'What time did he call you?'

'I'm sorry, I don't remember. It was late and I was about to go to bed.'

'You can't give us a time?'

'No, definitely not. It was over two weeks ago.'

'Herr Meiners,' Johann said, 'I'm guessing you don't get a call like that every night, do you? Let's have a think about this. What were you doing when the phone rang?'

'I was watching TV.'

'Then you probably remember what was on, don't you?'

'One of those boring whodunnits, I think. You know, piles of dead bodies – and that red-headed detective.'

'Was the programme over by the time our colleague called you?'

'Why do you want to know, anyway? Walter can tell you much better than me. He'd have noted—' He paused. 'What exactly is this about?'

'Routine questions,' Johann said in a bored tone. 'Had the programme finished?'

'Maybe. I'm not sure,' grumbled Lars Meiners.

Lena looked around the office. 'Would you mind if we sit down, please?'

'Why? Is there more to talk about?'

'I'd hardly ask for a seat if there wasn't,' Lena said with growing irritation. She gestured towards a table and chairs. 'If you wouldn't mind, Herr Meiners.'

Grudgingly, he followed the detectives over. Lena pulled a small recording device from her bag and placed it on the table. 'You don't object, do you?'

'What if I did?' asked Lars Meiners pointedly.

'No problem. We don't mind continuing this conversation at the station in Husum.'

'Switch it on then.'

Lena didn't need to be asked twice. 'You were about to rethink the question as to whether the TV programme was already over when our colleague called you.'

Lars Meiners cleared his throat. 'Like I said, I can't remember for certain. I think I'd just switched off the TV.'

'And how long had the TV been off?' asked Johann impatiently.

'Now, listen here, young man—' began Lars Meiners angrily, but he stopped short when he saw the look on Johann's face. 'All right, all right, I'm thinking. Yes, I'm pretty sure the programme had finished.'

'And what did you do afterwards?'

'What do you think? I went to bed – or was on my way, at least. Then the phone rang, and I left a little while after that.'

'*A little while?* What does that mean?'

'I've just about had it with all your questions. You're twisting my every word. I left to pick up the body. Isn't that enough?' Lars Meiners took a deep breath. 'Why are you asking me all this, dammit? I've done nothing wrong.'

'And no one says you have,' Lena said with a smile. 'We're just trying to get everything straight for our records. I'm sure you understand.'

'Yes, of course. I just don't remember the exact time – that's no crime, is it?'

'No, of course it isn't. I think we've narrowed down your departure time pretty well. It'll do for now. Who was at the beach when you arrived?'

'Walter Reimers, of course. And Dr Neumann.'

'You drove the hearse right up to the beach chair and transferred the body into the vehicle?'

'Yes, of course. That's my job!' Lars Meiners checked his watch. 'Is this going to take much longer? I've got things to do.'

'What did you do next?' asked Lena, ignoring his question.

'I drove back here and shifted Herr Bohlen into the refrigerated storage cabinet. And before you ask, after that I finally went to bed.'

'It must have been a long day for you,' Johann Grasmann said. 'Tell us, please, about the following day. Did Frau Bohlen come to see her husband one last time?'

'No, I went to see her the following morning to discuss the funeral arrangements. You know – date, coffin and all the rest.'

'How did Frau Bohlen seem to you? Sergeant Reimers had informed her of her husband's death the night before. How was she coping?'

Lars Meiners took his time. Eventually, he leaned back in his chair and said, 'They're always difficult, those visits right after a family member passes. You don't want to come at them like a salesman, but it has to be done. Sometimes the family finds it reassuring to do something practical: pick a nice coffin, discuss dates, organise the service.' Lena noticed that the funeral director was in his element now. 'You're asking about Frau Bohlen. She was still in shock, of course, but quite composed, given the circumstances – her husband had died unexpectedly in the night, after all. It's not like he was very old or very sick. Like I said, it was a good visit. We went over everything. That usually takes around an hour.'

'So you'd say Frau Bohlen's reaction was as per normal?' asked Johann.

'Yes, I would. She reacted like anyone else in such a difficult situation would. What more is there to add?' Lars Meiners flashed an irritated look at Johann as he said this.

'What did you do after your visit to Frau Bohlen?' asked Lena, drawing his attention back to herself.

'I washed and prepared Herr Bohlen that afternoon. The usual. Two days later, the police came to get him. But you already know that.'

'Did you notice anything unusual about the body?'

'No, and that's not my job. I'm a funeral director, not a coroner.'

'What did you do with his clothes?'

'Again, the usual. If the next of kin don't want them back – and generally, they don't – the clothes go to the Red Cross. They do regular pick-ups.'

'And how was it in this case?' asked Lena, struggling to remain calm.

'No idea. I'd have to check.'

'Then please go ahead and do so, Herr Meiners. It's important.'

The funeral director got up and went to his desk. He leafed through a folder and returned to the table. 'Just as I thought. Frau Bohlen didn't want the clothes.'

'And where are they now?' Johann couldn't sit still any longer. He jumped to his feet and leaned over Lars Meiners.

The funeral director shrank back and muttered, 'Picked up, I guess.'

Lena also stood up, and exchanged a look with her colleague. 'Perhaps we could take a look together, Herr Meiners,' she said calmly.

The three of them walked through the showroom. Lars Meiners opened a door at the back which led to a hallway with more doors leading off it. They entered a small room with four blue plastic sacks on the floor.

Johann pulled a pair of latex gloves from his pocket and snapped them on. Opening the first sack, he reached in carefully and pulled out a lady's shoe, which he put back in immediately. He opened the next sack and pulled out a man's dark-coloured cardigan, which he held out to Lars Meiners. The funeral director nodded. Johann Grasmann closed the bag again and lifted it out over the others.

'We need to take these,' Lena Lorenzen said. 'We'll give you a receipt.'

Lars Meiners had followed the search, his expression tense, and stammered, 'That . . . that won't be necessary.'

'It is for us,' Johann said, filling out the form and handing it to the funeral director. 'There you go.'

Slowly, Lars Meiners reached for the docket. 'And what happens now?'

Johann produced a cotton bud from a plastic container in his bag. 'We need a sample from you so we can identify your DNA on the clothes.' He handed the man the cotton bud. 'Run it along the inside of your cheek, please.'

Meiners took the cotton bud and did as Johann had asked.

'Right, that's us all finished here for now,' the young detective said. 'We'll be in touch if we have any further questions. Here's my card. Call us, please, if you think of anything else of interest.'

The funeral director walked them to the door and nodded in farewell.

Johann placed the blue sack in the boot then took his seat next to Lena and looked at his watch. 'So far, so good. Can you explain to me why people are always so suspicious when we interview them?'

'Must be you,' Lena said with a grin. 'Normally, I'm trustworthiness incarnate. The witnesses are putty in my hands.'

Johann smirked. 'Yeah, right.'

During their drive back to Norddorf, they talked about Johann's list of things to research and their plans for the next day. Lena dropped her colleague off at the house and drove back to Nebel. She'd rung her Aunt Beke over lunch and told her she'd be visiting later that afternoon.

Beke beamed when she opened the door. 'I'm so pleased you're here, *deern*.' They embraced warmly and Beke Althusen kissed her niece on both cheeks before leading her through into the large kitchen.

'Gosh, that smells good,' Lena said, suspecting that Beke had baked her favourite teatime treat. 'Let me guess – rhubarb cake?'

'It's a surprise!' Her aunt went to the stove and shifted a kettle on to the hotplate. 'I hope you'll have a cup of proper Amrum-style tea with me? Or are you addicted to coffee, like all the rest of them?'

Lena laughed. 'I wouldn't dream of asking for coffee in this house.'

'That's good. Our ancestors would turn in their graves.'

Lena loved her aunt's old Frisian house. Since she had taken the property over, more than thirty years ago, she'd undone many of the 'modernisations', as Beke called them. She'd removed the lino from over the flagstones, exchanged the cheap plastic windows for high-quality wooden ones, removed the post-war wallpaper and white-washed the walls instead. The ancient tiled stove had also been restored, even though Beke no longer used it. Bit by bit, she had returned the charm to the old house.

Beke placed the bowl of rock sugar on the table – an indispensable part of Frisian tea culture. Lena put one of the large crystals into her typical Frisian teacup and watched as Beke poured the hot tea. The cracking of the dissolving sugar stirred pleasant feelings of home and warmth in Lena's heart.

'It's been far too long,' she said and gave her aunt another hug.

'Easy, *deern*,' Beke said with a laugh, but Lena could tell how happy she was.

Beke served her niece a slice of rhubarb cake. 'Remember when the three of us used to sit here?' said Lena's aunt wistfully. Lena knew she was thinking of her sister. Lena's mother had died in one of the rare traffic accidents on Amrum. A car had hit her bicycle and Dorthe Lorenzen had run head-first into a tree. The driver had fled the scene and, by the time Dorthe was found, it had been too late. Lena was about to start her final year of high school, and her world collapsed. She had moved in with her Aunt Beke for several months following the accident.

'Now, tell me,' Beke said, 'where are you staying?'

'In the house of the old woman by the beach. That's what we used to call it as children.'

'Old Frau Schulte, you mean. Yes, she passed away about four years ago and left her house to the community. I heard it's been beautifully renovated.'

'Don't worry, it's not as beautiful as your house. But yes, it looks like the council spared no expense.'

'I read about it in the paper. An author stayed there for several months. The island's "writer-in-residence", they called him – apparently, he set one of his novels on the island. Bizarre, isn't it?'

'Why? If the book's a hit, what better publicity could there be for Amrum?'

'Do we really need more people here? In summer, I barely want to leave the house as it is.'

'You should visit Sylt some time – then you'd see real mass tourism. Amrum's still nice and quiet by comparison.'

'Still, I don't need all those people,' Beke said stubbornly.

'Maybe you don't, but what about all the other islanders who'd have had to move years ago without the tourists?' Lena laughed. 'You'd soon be the last resident on Amrum. And then how'd I get here without the ferry? I guess I could walk across the mudflats from Föhr at low tide.'

'Don't be silly, *deern*. You know what I mean. And if anyone tries to build any large hotels, I'll start up a – what do you call it? – local campaign.'

Lena couldn't help but smile. She had no trouble imagining her feisty aunt marching through Nebel waving a placard. 'I don't think you'll have to. The council has always wanted Amrum to keep its peaceful, quiet character. It's the island's main attraction.'

Beke Althusen sighed. 'Let's hope you're right. Peace and quiet is exactly what I want in my last few remaining years.'

'*Last few remaining years?*' said Lena indignantly. 'Don't even think about it. I need you for at least another twenty years.' She leaned over and kissed Beke's cheek. 'Not to mention your rhubarb cake.'

Beke laughed heartily. 'But especially the cake, hey?'

Lena turned serious. 'No, Beke. Just you.'

The old woman nodded and looked down at her teacup, her cheeks slightly flushed. Hesitantly, she said, 'Are you sure you don't want—?'

'No!' Lena said, cutting her off. 'Why would I want to see him? And I certainly don't want to meet that woman.'

'You could meet here.'

Lena looked at her aunt. How many times had she told Beke over the years that she wanted nothing to do with her father? And yet her aunt mentioned him every time they met. In Lena's eyes, her father was partially to blame for her mother's death. A few months before the accident, her mother had found out that her father had been cheating on her with the same woman for years. On the day she died, they had had a big argument and Lena's mother had stormed out of the house. The accident had happened a few minutes later. One year down the line, the other woman had moved in with her father.

'Please leave it, Beke. You know how I feel about this.'

'My dear child, your father may have made mistakes, but he's still your father.'

'You must give me the recipe for the rhubarb cake sometime. I might even have a go on my next day off. What do you think – would I manage?'

'You can do anything if you put your mind to it,' Beke replied with a smile.

'Great, perhaps I'll surprise Joe. He won't believe his eyes. Though maybe I should do a trial run first.'

'How is Joe?' asked Beke.

'Great! Yep, he's doing just fine.'

'Do you two have plans for the future?'

Lena grinned. 'I'm going to be chief constable and Joe's going to be my PA.' Beke said nothing and refilled their cups. 'Joe wants us to move in together,' Lena said eventually.

'And you don't?'

There was a pause while Lena considered her reply. 'I like things the way they are. If we move in together, next thing you know he'll want to get married, and then . . .' Lena faltered.

'He wants children?'

'I think so. Three or four, I'm guessing.'

'Did he tell you that?'

'Not in so many words. And to be honest, I'm not ready to talk about it. Neither about the one thing nor the other. Especially not about children.'

Beke nodded slowly. Lena knew how much her aunt had wanted children. After four miscarriages, her doctor had advised her to go on the pill.

'Not right now, anyway,' Lena added. 'My job is more important right now.'

Beke placed her hands on top of Lena's. '*Deern*, you still have time. If you're not ready yet, you shouldn't do it.'

9

Lena linked arms with Beke. They were walking towards the shore of the Wadden Sea after talking at the kitchen table for another hour.

'Tell me, Beke, what do people say about the children's home in Norddorf?'

'Getting down to business now, are we?' Beke said with a smile. 'Things have been rather quiet in that direction lately. But I'm an old woman and don't hear much gossip any more. There may be more going on there than I know about.'

Lena pricked up her ears. 'And what have you heard about in the past?'

'People talk a lot – doesn't mean it's all true.'

'Go on, tell,' Lena demanded.

'All right, all right. Well, in the beginning, when the house was being converted, folk worried about the problem kids who'd be coming to the island. And the police did in fact have to chase after some of the older boys a few times, though apparently they never got any further than the ferry, or Dagebüll at most. Probably nothing that doesn't happen at other children's care homes. People soon calmed down.'

'But something else happened?' asked Lena.

'Well . . . according to some, one summer – the home had been open for a few years by then – a young holidaymaker was raped in Norddorf, not far from the home. You can imagine what people were saying – that it could only have been one of the older boys from the home. But the police never found anyone, not least because the girl had nothing to say about her alleged rapist.'

'I'll see what I can find in the records.'

'That was years ago, and you know how busy this place gets over the holiday season.'

Lena nodded. She sensed that Beke had something else to tell her. 'But that wasn't the only piece of gossip you picked up?'

By now they'd reached the track that ran along the eastern shore of the island. Beke stopped and looked out at the Wadden Sea. 'I love it just here.' She said nothing for a while. Two seagulls flew out over the mudflats, screeching. 'Maybe we should let those old rumours lie. Folk talk too much.' After one look at Lena, however, she continued. 'Apparently, there weren't many children at the home during the first year – not all of the places were taken up. The big house and the renovations must have cost a fortune – anyone could work that out. Gossip started up again and people wondered where all the money was coming from, especially since the home wasn't running to capacity. Folk were saying that big black limousines visited the home at night. A load of nonsense, if you ask me. Where were they supposed to have come from? Flown in by helicopter at night? We're still on an island, after all.' Beke shook her head scornfully. 'Once the future Frau Bohlen came to the home, the tittle-tattle soon stopped, and it also helped that Herr Bohlen became active in one or two clubs. That's what folk are like. You know – anyone new to the island gets viewed with suspicion and the wildest tales go round.'

'And now that Hein Bohlen is dead – what are people saying now?'

'Nothing at first, but once word got out that his body had been taken to the mainland for a post-mortem, the rumours started flying again. I haven't been listening, I'm afraid. The poor man is dead and we shouldn't be speaking ill of him.'

Lena nodded in agreement and changed the subject. They walked on for a little while, only turning back when dark clouds began to gather on the horizon.

'How long are you staying on Amrum, *deern*?' asked Beke when they said their goodbyes.

'Not sure yet. A few days or a week, perhaps. I'll drop by again soon.' Lena grinned. 'And then you simply have to teach me how to bake that rhubarb cake, OK?'

They embraced for a long moment. Beke gave her niece a kiss on the cheek and waved a teary-eyed farewell. Lena sighed as she steered the Passat back on to the main road. She would have liked to spend the evening with Beke. She decided to stay at her aunt's for a day or two, once the case was solved or scrapped.

Pulling up outside the beach house, she took out her phone and called Superintendent Warnke. He picked up on the second ring. Lena brought him up to speed in as few words as possible.

'Any news from Hamburg?' she asked.

'You'd be the first to know.'

'I urgently need the list of phones connected to the network that night between nine p.m. and midnight. I also need Bohlen's phone records from his last two days – or better yet, the whole week.'

'I'd expected you to ask for the former, and it's already set up. You should get the data tomorrow. Bohlen's phone records shouldn't take much longer.'

'Great. What about a search warrant for the home and his flat?'

'On what grounds? We have nothing solid, you know that. But I'll try – I can't promise anything, though.'

'Any chance of getting a look at Walter Reimers' personnel file?'

DSU Warnke groaned. 'I'll try. But don't get carried away again.'

'I won't,' Lena replied firmly, choosing not to comment on the 'again'. 'I need a court order for the tax office. We need access to the documents relating to the purchase of the property.'

'That should be doable. I'll email you in the morning.'

'Thanks. I'll call again tomorrow night.'

Her next phone call was to her retired friend and father figure, Enno Eilts, DSU Warnke's predecessor.

'I don't have much for you,' he said after their warm greeting. 'How are you getting on?' Lena told him briefly what they'd uncovered so far. 'Walter Reimers. The name sounds familiar.'

'He's been stationed on the island for eight years. That's all I know.'

'I'm sure he's never worked in Kiel – Schleswig, perhaps. I'll call someone there and get back to you if I find anything. But as to my not having much for you, I did some asking around. Not that easy when you've been out of the game for a while. I feel like I spent hours talking with my old colleagues about my retirement and how I'm coping with it. I could hardly get straight to the point. No one's become particularly chummy with Warnke. "Overambitious" was about the nicest description. No one seemed to know much about your case, which I couldn't mention explicitly, of course, only that he's been keeping out of all current investigations almost entirely. In other words, he's busy with something else. If I'm not mistaken, things suddenly got very quiet around Warnke following the death of the director of this children's home.'

'Strange. Sounds as though whatever's going on is taking up all his attention.'

'Or he's got the wind up because he's involved somehow. I wouldn't put it past him.'

'Then why would he kick up such a fuss? I can't really believe the Flensburg office would have begged him for help.'

Enno Eilts sighed. 'I agree. Something's up, and it seems to me like you're an important pawn in this game. Please look after yourself. I have a bad feeling about all this.'

'I know. I'll be careful.'

They said their goodbyes and Lena next called Ben, her colleague from Flensburg.

'*Moin*, Lena. I've been expecting you to call.'

'I'm sorry, Ben. I've been flat out.'

'How are you getting on with our boy?'

'All good so far. Positively surprised, even.'

'He's nobody's fool,' Ben Baier said. 'But watch out – he's apparently on very good terms with the boss.'

'Will do. Thanks. Have you heard anything else?'

'Not really. No one else was asked if they'd like to take on the case. The boss decided on his own. And you know he's constantly in touch with your Warnke. That's all I've heard.'

'That information alone speaks volumes.'

'Are you making any progress?'

'I think so. But you can imagine what it's like when you don't start investigating until two weeks after the fact.'

'Absolutely. But I know you – you'll give it your all and solve the case sooner or later. When can I see you again?'

Ben's question had come out of nowhere. Lena swallowed and took a deep breath. 'I don't think your wife would be too impressed, would she?'

There was a silence before he replied. 'That didn't stop you two years ago.'

'Ben, we both needed someone that night. I thought we agreed—'

'It's all right, Lena,' Ben said. 'I know. Pity, though.' There was another pause, then he added, 'I just can't forget that night.'

'You must. For your own sake as well as for your family,' said Lena, quickly adding, 'and for mine too.'

After their one-night stand she'd been on the point of calling Ben or driving over to Flensburg many times, but on each occasion had been stopped by the thought of his wife and two young children. Eventually, she'd sought refuge in her relationship with Joe and tried to forget Ben.

'You're right, of course,' he said quietly. After another pause he added, 'I'll be in touch. Look after yourself – and our young man.'

'Thanks for your support, Ben.'

'No trouble at all. I honestly don't mind.'

'I know. Thank you anyway.'

'Will you call me?'

'Bye, Ben.'

Lena waited until he hung up. Ben's words still rang in her ears. He'd sounded honest, wistful. Lena tried to swallow the lump in her throat. She'd asked Ben for help on the spur of the moment, but had known it was a mistake the moment she'd called him. Lena stared at her phone. Deep in thought, she next called Leon.

'Yeah?' he said, as always, answering the phone without giving his name.

'Got anything for me?'

'That's for you to judge.'

'Spill!'

'His regular email account is boring as hell. Just the usual. I'll send you a link with his emails from the last twelve months.'

'OK. What else?'

'The home network was extremely well secured. Too well, I'd say.'

'Strange.'

'I agree. The guy had another email account, with Gmail. He must have had it a while because it still has the old-style ending.'

'Anything of interest?'

'Completely empty. He must have deleted all his emails. I couldn't find a thing.'

'So why would he do that? If he didn't use the account, he could have just closed it.'

'He did use it, though, but I only found the faintest traces on his hard drive. I tried, honestly, but there was no way to recover those emails. I assume he always deleted them immediately from his inbox as well as his sent items folder.'

'That's odd,' Lena said. 'Could he have saved anything to the cloud?'

'I found only a very few, very well-covered tracks on his PC. I'd say he was extremely careful – either he knew what he was doing or he was very lucky. I'm guessing the former. But I'll have another look tomorrow. I hate not being able to find anything. Everyone's got a skeleton in the closet – even you.'

'Call me if you find anything. I may need some records from the tax office.'

Leon groaned. 'You're not asking for much, are you?'

'I *may* need them, I said. I'll be in touch.'

Lena hung up and climbed out of the Passat. In the house, Johann was sitting at the kitchen table with his laptop. She fetched a bottle of water and a glass and joined him.

'Any luck?' she asked.

'Everyone had already finished up for the day at the tax office in Leck.'

'OK, well, we'll have the court order in the morning. We may need you then to travel to the mainland, unless we ask the local police to help out. Maybe even a phone call will do the trick. Let's wait and see.'

'Next we have the three ladies. First up, Sabine Bohlen, née Lauer. She came to the island six years ago and married Hein Bohlen three years later. She studied in Münster. She's turning forty-two this year, no children. Born and raised in the Cloppenburg district of Bösel. Catholic. Both parents still alive, no siblings. Before moving to Amrum, she worked in several different places across northern Germany: Münster, Oldenburg, Bremen, Norderstedt. No criminal record.'

'Is she still a member of the Church?'

'According to the records, yes. Unless she left a few days ago.'

'Nothing else?'

'I'm not sure if it's important, but she was off work for a whole year. I'm guessing she was on sick leave. She wasn't receiving any benefits.'

'For a whole year? Let's pay her another visit today. I've got a few more questions for her of my own. I don't believe in this happy marriage she was trying to sell us. OK, what about Isabel Müller?'

'She's twenty-five years old. Both parents died in a car crash when she was twelve. She spent the following years in homes across northern Germany.'

'Both parents?' asked Lena, shocked, thinking of her own mother. 'Both at the same time?'

'Yes, or she wouldn't have ended up in a home. She had a brother, three years younger. They were put in the same home at first and then separated later.'

'Why?'

'Can't find anything in the records, but the way she was shifted from home to home, I'm guessing she was trouble. She was finally placed with a foster family at fourteen and stayed there until she was eighteen. After graduating from high school, she studied in Hamburg. Completed her probationary year at a youth centre in Rostock then returned to Hamburg as a fieldworker for children's social services.'

'What about her brother?'

'He passed away a year and a half ago.'

'Another accident?'

'I couldn't find anything on it. Would you like me to . . . ?'

'Yes please, if you could.'

Johann checked his files. 'Oldenburg in Niedersachsen. That's where he was last. I know someone at the station there. I'll give him a call in the morning.'

'Anything else about Isabel Müller?'

'She's been working at the home for a little over six months, like she told us. Unmarried; no children.'

'Can you please email me the list of homes she was placed in?'

'I'm on to it. I'll send it through together with today's report.'

'Great. What about her predecessor, Anna . . . ?'

'Bauer. Anna Bauer. I found her entry in the register of residents on Amrum. She de-registered when she moved away and her new address is on Mallorca. How would you like me to proceed?'

'Try the Spanish consulate in Hamburg tomorrow. I'd really like to speak to her.'

'Do you think she's a suspect?'

'Call it a gut feeling. She works at the home for five years and then suddenly quits without giving any notice. And Sabine Bohlen hasn't the faintest idea why – even though they worked side by side on a daily basis.'

'OK, I'll try the consulate tomorrow. Anna Bauer is thirty-five, originally from Bavaria . . .' He checked his notes. 'Regensburg. That's also where she studied before moving first to North Rhine-Westphalia for work, and then to Amrum. Also unmarried and no children.'

'From Amrum to Mallorca. I doubt she's working in a home over there.'

'Maybe she's an entertainer at one of the resorts. I've heard they like teachers for the job. Or she's just taking some time out?'

'Pure speculation. We need her phone number and then we'll soon find out.' Lena checked the time. 'Almost eight. OK, I think that's enough for today.'

'What's the plan for tomorrow?' asked Johann.

'Talk to the cook and the rest of the staff. A few more questions for Sabine Bohlen. The tax office in Leck. And then we have the list of Hein Bohlen's friends and associates.'

'OK. We don't have anything so far. Not surprising, considering we don't even know whether Hein Bohlen's death was murder. Not to mention *how* he was murdered.'

'I don't reckon things are that bad. Tomorrow is another day.'

Lena's phone buzzed. She checked the display. A text from Erck.

10

'Do you still drink Martini on ice?'

Lena had walked into the Norddorf Strandhalle a few minutes ago and found Erck waiting for her at a table by the window.

He'd handed her the Martini as soon as she sat down.

'Every now and then,' she said.

He raised his glass. 'This time it's official: welcome to Amrum!' She sipped at her drink. 'How long has it been?' asked Erck.

'Fourteen years,' Lena replied.

Erck sighed. 'That's quite a while.'

'How did you get hold of my number?'

'Beke. It took a bit of doing, but she succumbed to my charms in the end. Don't be angry with her – she likes me. And what else was I supposed to do? You know I'm bad at waiting.'

'What are you up to these days?' Lena asked, to change the subject.

'I manage holiday-home rentals, and it's going pretty well. Many of the local homeowners have given up living on Amrum or become too old to look after guests. These days the season runs from before Easter until mid- to late October.'

'What else?'

He raised both hands and twisted them back and forth. 'No ring. I couldn't convince any woman to take me. And you? Ringlessly happy too?'

Lena rolled her eyes. 'Stop it, Erck. Beke would have told you long ago if I'd done anything like that. No, I'm not married and nor am I planning to be any time soon.'

'Does that mean I'm still in with a chance?'

Lena had to smile in spite of herself. Erck hadn't changed at all. 'Long-distance relationships aren't really my thing.'

He sighed theatrically. 'Unless the crime rate here suddenly went through the roof and Schleswig-Holstein's only competent detective was permanently required.'

Lena drained her Martini. 'I can't stay long. I still have work to do.'

She could tell by Erck's eyes that he was disappointed. 'What a shame,' he said. 'Just a few more minutes for an old friend? One more Martini?'

Lena shrugged. 'But only one more.'

Erck signalled the waitress to bring two more drinks. When he turned back to Lena, their eyes met. 'Dammit,' he said quietly. 'I've missed you.'

Lena swallowed. 'That was another life. One that's long over.' Her voice was almost a whisper.

'You could have called.'

'And then what?' asked Lena. 'Would it have made it any easier for you?'

'Anything would have been better than your silence.'

Lena closed her eyes for a moment. She didn't want to tell Erck how many times she'd picked up the phone and how close she'd come to ringing him but had always decided against it at the very last moment.

'I couldn't call you, Erck, let alone visit you here.'

'As you said, it's long over.'

Their Martinis arrived. Lena raised the glass this time. 'I'm sorry, Erck. I didn't want to hurt you, but I know I did.'

He tried to smile. Then he got up and moved his chair right alongside hers. 'Do you remember how we never wanted to sit opposite each other? People used to look sideways at us when we sat next to each other like this.' He raised his glass and chinked it against hers. 'To us!'

'To us,' Lena repeated.

◆ ◆ ◆

Lena got back to the house around ten. After the third Martini, Erck had told her some more about the last few years on Amrum. Aside from the holiday rentals, he also gave surfing lessons. Two years ago he'd bought an old house in Norddorf and renovated it from the ground up. He'd done most of the work himself over the winter months, and now, finally, he said, his house was no longer a building site. Erck's goodnight hug had left her breathless for a moment. Neither of them had let go for what felt like an eternity.

Lena opened up her laptop to check her emails. Johann had sent his report through and there was an email from Superintendent Warnke. She opened it and was amazed to find not only the court order for the tax office attached, but also a copy of Reimers' personnel file.

'That was quick,' Lena murmured.

Warnke must have found a judge willing to issue the order that evening. Lena was astonished that he'd gained access to the personnel file this fast.

She opened the file and scanned through Reimers' history. Enno Eilts had guessed right. Reimers had been stationed in Schleswig for eleven years before applying for the position on Amrum. Previous to Schleswig, he'd worked in Hamburg, where he'd been demoted by one rank. From the vaguely worded summary, Lena assumed that he'd cultivated close contacts with the criminal milieu and passed on classified information. The internal investigation had concluded with the decision to demote Reimers. Lena guessed that he'd been shielded from worse by his superior officer. She noted down the name of the station.

If she made an official inquiry, she wouldn't get a reply for weeks, if at all. She reached for her phone and called Leon.

'Yeah?'

'Hi, Leon. I need a report from the department of internal investigations.'

Leon laughed drily. 'You want me to hack your own guys? Funny!'

'Hamburg police. It'll be years before they give me anything.'

She gave him Reimers' details and explained the situation briefly.

'That'll take hours. And what if they haven't even digitised the bloody report?'

'You can't get in?'

'Getting in isn't the problem. Not getting seen is.'

'So?'

'Dammit, Lena, I think we're just about even again. Just because you did me a favour that one time—'

'As I remember correctly, I saved you from several years behind bars.'

'You know very well that my partner tried to pin everything on me.'

'Yes or no?'

'Police. What next – FBI? Pentagon?'

Lena said nothing.

'I'll try,' Leon said eventually. 'But I need time. One night at least. I'll have to . . . never mind. You don't care anyway.'

'Thanks, Leon,' Lena said, but he'd already hung up. She sighed. He was right. She'd demanded his help several times over the last couple of years without offering anything in return. She assumed Leon would be asking for some service in kind pretty soon or refuse to come to her aid again.

Lena turned her attention to the personnel file. It sounded as though not everyone in Schleswig had been a fan of Reimers either. One of his colleagues had made a complaint about the rude tone he used with female subordinates. They'd held a mediation session and

Reimers had vowed to mend his ways. Lena texted Enno Eilts with the news that Reimers had indeed worked in Schleswig – with a bit of luck, Enno would find someone who knew more than the file offered.

There was nothing of interest in the rest of Reimers' history. Lena closed the email and opened Johann's report. She skimmed through the facts and focussed on the homes Isabel Müller had been placed in as a child. When she compared them with the list from Hein Bohlen's employers, she found they'd never been at the same home. She decided to question the teacher again once they knew more about the circumstances of her brother's death.

Lastly, she clicked on the link Leon had sent her. It led to over a thousand emails from Hein Bohlen's inbox over the last twelve months. Lena groaned and started with the messages from the weeks preceding his death. The director had exchanged emails with children's services at various local authorities, with tradesmen who'd done work at the home, with his accountant and a few others who had a connection with the home in one way or another. Lena scanned the subject lines of several hundred emails and found nothing relevant to her investigation. Then she opened the file with the deleted emails Leon had found. Aside from five uninteresting emails, there was a brief message from a certain Herbert Bergendorf dated five days before Hein Bohlen's death. It read:

We need to speak urgently!

Lena searched the list of associates Sabine Bohlen had given them. The name wasn't on it. Hein Bohlen hadn't replied to the email. Lena logged on to the police database and searched for Herbert Bergendorf. She noted down one address in Hamburg and one on Amrum.

Checking the time, she was surprised to find it was nearly one in the morning. She closed the laptop down and went to bed.

◆　◆　◆

'Morning,' said Johann when Lena came into the kitchen. 'Coffee?'

'Black and strong, please.'

'Poor night's sleep?'

'The mattress is too soft,' Lena muttered and took the mug Johann was handing her. 'How about yourself? Been up long?'

'Not too long,' he said. 'I've been checking a few things. Was my report OK?'

Lena took a long sip of her coffee. 'All good. The court order for the tax office has come through, along with Reimers' personnel file.'

Johann whistled appreciatively. 'Wow! Who'd have thought? And what does it say?'

Lena filled him in briefly on what she'd learned from the file.

'The properly interesting bits are off limits, of course. I guess there's no chance of getting our hands on those.'

'Wait and see,' Lena said with a smile.

'You've got an idea?'

'Like I said, wait and see.'

Johann nodded. 'OK.'

'I'll ring the tax office soon. Did you find out what programme the funeral director watched that night?'

'The only whodunnit on that evening finished at quarter past eleven.' Johann grinned. 'And it was the detective with the red hair.'

'So if the funeral director watched the programme to the end, then Reimers called him later.'

'That's right! And Meiners said he was on his way to bed. We were right: there are at least twenty minutes unaccounted for.'

'We need the phone records ASAP,' Lena said. 'Do we know yet if Hein Bohlen actually went to the supermarket on his last day?'

'I'm on to it. And I'll send his clothes to Forensics in Flensburg. With a bit of luck, they'll get back to us the day after tomorrow. I'll make sure they know it's urgent.' Johann handed Lena the basket of bread rolls and pastries. She picked a croissant, dunked it into her coffee and took a bite.

'I saw my aunt yesterday. She told me a holidaymaker was raped here a few years back. Apparently, the older boys from the home came under suspicion. Can you ask for the file?'

'Will do. We're meeting the cook at ten, and I've asked the two casual staff to come in fifteen minutes later. What are we going to do with Frau Bohlen's list?'

'We'll split it between us. Ring everyone first, then decide who we need to see in person. And I've got someone else to add to the list. We'll see him first.'

When Johann looked at her expectantly, she added, 'A chance hit.'

After getting redirected twice on the phone to the tax office, Lena finally managed to speak with the director, Nils Oppen.

'I need some info about a property purchase on Amrum,' she explained. 'I gather you've received the court order?'

'Yes, Inspector,' the man on the phone said quickly, 'and I've had the documents relating to the case sent to my office. What would you like to know?'

'The house was largely paid for out of private funds. What statements were made by the buyer regarding those funds?'

Lena could hear pages being turned. After a long few moments, Nils Oppen cleared his throat and said, 'Herr Bohlen stated that he'd won the money on the lottery.'

'And you have proof?'

'Yes, of course. I have a statement from the Niedersachsen lottery company attesting to a win of eight hundred thousand euros. The precise amount is—'

'Can you scan and email the statement to me?'

'That should be possible if you give me your official CID address. But I can't promise it'll be today. I'll get the ball rolling as soon as I can.'

Lena groaned inwardly. She had neither the time nor the patience for the pace of a provincial tax office.

'Did your office have the authenticity of the certificate attested?' she asked pointedly.

Nils Oppen appeared to leaf through his files again. 'Looks as though it was accepted as is, but that's not unusual. The statement looks fine to me.'

'I'm guessing that means you deal with similar statements on a regular basis?' Lena sounded annoyed.

'No, I don't. This was a first.'

'That's what I thought. I think someone put one over on you.'

'How do you mean?'

'Herr Oppen, I assure you that it's in your best interests to clear this up as fast as possible. We're dealing with a serious murder investigation here.'

'Of course, Inspector—'

'Great,' Lena said, cutting him off. 'Then I suggest you find out whether Herr Bohlen really did win the lottery as soon as you can. I'm sure you don't need another court order, do you?'

'You mean—?'

'I mean you pick up the phone right now and sort the matter out. Can I count on you?' Lena's voice had become increasingly sharp.

'Of course you can,' the director of the tax office said after a moment's hesitation.

'Call me as soon as you have the result – you have my number. And I also want the contact details of the lottery company.'

'Hanover. They're in Hanover.'

'I'll expect to hear from you shortly.'

Moments after she'd finished the call, her phone rang. It was Leon.

'It wasn't easy. Last night's gonna cost you,' he said without greeting. 'The files are in your inbox.'

He hung up before Lena could say anything.

She opened her laptop and studied the files Leon had sent. Just as she'd thought. Reimers had been involved in a corruption scandal. His name had been found on a list during a raid on well-known criminals. The list assigned large sums of cash against each name. Nothing could be proven in the course of the following investigations into Reimers, neither him accepting the bribe nor any services given in return. When no principal witness could be found, Reimers agreed to his demotion by one rank. There were, on the other hand, several breaches of conduct that could be proven – protocols that disappeared without trace, unjustified violence during preliminary arrests and manipulation of witness statements. The investigators also judged Reimers to be of unsound character and suspected a gambling addiction.

Lena couldn't believe Reimers had been allowed to stay in the police force following such serious allegations. Clearly, he'd had friends in high places who had protected him and made his transfer to another region possible.

But that was many years ago. At this point, Lena couldn't see a connection with her current case. She hoped the phone data would be more conclusive.

Next, she googled Herbert Bergendorf, the email contact from Hein Bohlen's digital recycling bin. The man was in his seventies and before his retirement he had been CEO of a large bank in Hamburg, and in this capacity had been active in countless organisations and charitable institutions. Her search yielded a huge number of results. Aside from his holiday home on Amrum, he owned a mansion in Hamburg's most exclusive neighbourhood.

Lena looked at her watch. Half an hour before they'd have to leave for the children's home. She leaned back and closed her eyes, feeling guilty that she hadn't called Joe sooner. She grabbed her phone to call him.

'Hi, Lena,' he said when he picked up. 'How are you?'

'I'm fine.'

'Glad to hear it. Seen your aunt yet?'

'Yes, yesterday afternoon. She says hello.'

'Hello back. Tell her I'd love to see her in Kiel again soon. Maybe we could plan something nice together, a day trip or something. What do you think?'

'Sure, why not?'

'How long will you have to stay on Amrum?' he asked after a few moments of silence.

'It's complicated. Too soon to tell. A few more days at least.'

'I guess you're in a hurry?' asked Joe.

'Yep, the next interview's at ten.'

'Keep in touch?'

'Sure.'

'Look after yourself, Lena.'

'Will do.'

'Later then,' Joe said, and Lena could hear the disappointment in his voice. 'My phone's always on. Call when you get a chance.'

'All right, Joe. Catch you later.'

Lena hung up and stared at her phone for a while before forcing herself to get up.

11

On the drive over to the children's home Johann told Lena what he'd found out in the meantime. His colleague in Oldenburg had reported that Isabel Müller's brother had committed suicide eighteen months earlier. He'd been a regular patient at Karl Jaspers Hospital, a specialist psychiatric unit. The inquiry into his death had ruled out third-party involvement. No suicide letter had been found.

The Spanish consulate in Hamburg had been most cooperative and handed over Anna Bauer's current address. Turned out she really did work as an entertainer at a large resort complex. Johann had tried to call her but not got through. He'd try again in the afternoon.

'Bohlen's visit to the supermarket is confirmed. I spoke with the manager. He knows Bohlen and even spoke with him that day.'

'Did he notice anything?'

'That's what I asked. He said no at first, but then he said Bohlen seemed rather nervous.'

'Interesting. Anything unusual about the shopping trip?'

'Yes, I'd actually noticed from the receipt already. The shop would have done for a family of four, but a normal shop for the home should have been much bigger. The manager confirmed that the home usually spends around six hundred euros per shop. What Hein Bohlen bought on that day was minimal by comparison. Either he wasn't in the right frame of mind or he didn't have the time, or both.'

'More evidence suggesting that Bohlen wasn't fully himself. We need to find out who else he saw that day. I'm hoping the phone records will give us a clue.'

Just as they reached the children's home, Lena's phone rang. It was the man from the tax office.

'I had the statement checked,' he reported dutifully. 'It appears that the document was indeed falsified.'

'Easy as that,' Lena muttered.

'Well, no – a simple case of human error. But the case officer has been retired for years and, as I just found out, passed away not long ago.'

'So what happens now?'

'We'll request new documentation from the home's beneficiaries, although the whole affair may fall under the statute of limitations. Nothing like this has ever happened during my career up until now.'

'Would you please send the documents to CID Kiel, marked for the attention of Lena Lorenzen?'

'Of course, Inspector.'

Lena said goodbye and hung up. 'Great. Now we know for certain that Bohlen's money was dodgy, but that doesn't get us any further.'

'An important clue, though,' Johann said. 'I'm sure we'll tie up the loose ends over the course of the investigation. I'm guessing the cash withdrawals have something to do with it. Repayments? Bit late, though, isn't it?'

Lena nodded and asked, 'What's the cook's name?'

Johann opened his little notebook. 'Rosa Behrens.'

Lena, who'd been about to climb out of the car, fell back into her seat. 'Age?'

'Thirty-four. Why?'

'Unless I'm much mistaken, we went to school together. You could even say we were friends for a while as children.'

'And now?'

'Not these days. But if you get the feeling she'll only open up to me, be ready to make another important phone call, yes?'

Johann nodded as they got out and walked to the house.

Sabine Bohlen accompanied them to the large dining room of the children's home. A woman came out of the adjacent kitchen, untying her apron. She smiled when she saw Lena and held out her hand. 'Even as a child you always used to play cops and robbers with the boys.'

Lena grinned. 'I can't believe you remember that.'

'That and a whole lot besides. But that's not why you're here.'

Sabine Bohlen had followed their exchange with growing surprise. Now she stepped forward. 'I'll be in my office if you need me.'

'Thank you, Frau Bohlen. Yes, we'd like to speak with you again once we've finished here.'

Sabine left the room without reacting to Lena's comment.

Rosa Behrens pulled out a chair. 'Would you like to take a seat?'

Lena nodded and gestured for Johann to sit too.

'So, what can I do for you?' asked Rosa.

Lena looked at her childhood friend. She wouldn't have recognised Rosa immediately. She'd been a short, chubby eight-year-old but there was no trace of that now. She was as tall as Lena, slim and very pretty. Her long black hair was pinned up these days, but her smile was the same and her eyes shone with the same greenish hazel as twenty-five years ago.

'As you know, we're here about your boss's death. What we're mainly interested in is whether you noticed anything unusual in the weeks and especially days before.'

'I thought you might ask that. I would have said no if you'd put me on the spot, but I've thought it over since and I think I did notice something. Hein had been somewhat unfocussed lately. I can't think of a better way of putting it. In hindsight, I feel like he was walking around in a daze at times, as if he was on another planet, but not all the time. That's why it didn't stand out to me at first. It came in waves.

Like, suddenly, as if he'd just thought of something, he was miles away. I know it sounds weird, but that's the best way I can describe it.'

'It's all right, Rosa. Just tell us how you saw it – that would be the most help.'

'I mean, he'd always had a temper, but he had it under control. You know how my father—' The cook glanced at Johann and then back at Lena. 'How can I put it? He wasn't an easy person. If you've lived with someone like that since you're a kid, you kind of get a sense for people with anger issues.'

'Do you have any idea why he might have behaved that way?'

'We weren't that close.'

Lena sensed that her former friend wasn't telling everything. She glanced at Johann, who was writing notes in his book.

'I'm pretty much always in the kitchen. I didn't use to go for the groceries either. I've only been doing the shopping since . . .' She seemed to be looking for the right words. 'Well, since he's no longer been around. Before, he always used to do it himself.'

Johann rose. 'I left something in the car.'

'No problem,' Lena said. 'We'll carry on without you.'

Rosa continued once he'd left the room. 'There was a time when we had more to do with each other. I hate to speak ill of the dead, but it's probably better if I tell you everything.'

'It'll stay between us, if you'd rather.'

'Yes, please. At the end of the day, I like it here. It's better than working in hospitality, where the hours are shocking. Never mind. Hein Bohlen: the long and short of it is, he chased after me.'

'What happened?'

Rosa Behrens rubbed her hands and took a deep breath. 'Please keep it to yourself if possible. You know how it goes. Suddenly, the boss spends more time in the kitchen, talks to you, a bit overly familiar and considerate. I didn't think anything of it at first – I mean, he was newly married. I didn't take it seriously, not even when he touched me, you know, like accidentally brushing against me. I guess it was my mistake too. Not nipping it in the bud. I don't know.'

Lena waited patiently for her old school friend to get to the interesting part. She knew from experience that she needed to hold back at this point.

'It happened one morning. The kids were out of the house; Frau Bohlen and Anna were shopping. I was in the kitchen prepping the lunch, like every day. He came in and asked if he could help. Of course he didn't need to, but he stayed anyway. He talked and talked. I think I stopped listening at some point. Next thing I know he's behind me, pressing himself against me and kissing my neck. I probably don't need to explain to you what his hands were doing.'

Lena could tell how difficult it was for Rosa to talk about the incident. Her hands moved nervously around the tabletop, her cheeks were flushed and she avoided eye contact with Lena.

'I froze. I mean, you read about things like that happening but it's never happened to me before. He probably saw it as his cue to keep going. He pulled up my skirt and . . .' Rosa Behrens faltered. Lena leaned forward and placed her hand on top of hers.

'At last I reacted, shoved him off me and . . .' She swallowed. 'I ran out of the kitchen. He caught up with me in the hallway. No, not like you think. He apologised over and over, swearing that he hadn't meant to upset me. It was probably wrong of me to keep quiet about it. I don't know. I mean, nothing happened, or almost nothing. Or at least that's what I told myself. I really wanted to keep my job. I like it here – apart from that one incident . . .'

While Rosa was talking, she kept glancing at the door, expecting Lena's colleague back at any moment.

Lena picked up her phone. 'I'll text Johann to start interviewing the casual staff. Then we'll have a little more time to ourselves.'

Rosa looked relieved. 'I guess you'll understand that I didn't exactly seek out his company after that,' she continued. 'He never tried it on again. Not with me, at least.' Lena looked at her expectantly. 'I really can't say. Like I said, I'm always in the kitchen. I honestly don't know if he's done it to anyone else.'

'Can you remember exactly when this happened?'

'Of course! It was a year after he got married – almost to the day. Mid-May. I don't know the exact date but it was a Tuesday. Is that close enough?'

'Yes, thanks. In any case, it's no longer relevant from a legal perspective now that Hein Bohlen is dead. But back to your co-workers. Did you ever notice anything that might suggest he molested someone else? Anna Bauer quit without notice. Do you think he might have tried it on with her?'

'I swear I'd tell you, Lena, but I just don't know.' She sighed. 'Maybe I didn't want to know. Ever since the incident two years ago . . . Well, I try to focus on my work rather than on my co-workers. Anna never said anything but, then again, I was off sick when she upped and left. I didn't even get a chance to say goodbye – that's how fast it all happened.'

'And Isabel Müller? Do you think he . . . ?'

'Maybe. I did notice how he was with her. It reminded me a little of my situation two years ago. But she's a tough woman. She told me once that she does martial arts – don't ask me to remember which one, though. He would've got himself a black eye.' She halted, considering the meaning of her words. 'But I don't think she had anything to do with his death.'

'It's all right, Rosa. I know how you meant it. I'm afraid I have to ask you where you were on the night of Bohlen's death.'

She grinned. 'I need an alibi? Exciting. Well, if I remember correctly, I was at a birthday party. Do you need names?'

'If possible, please. And a phone number.'

'Sure thing. So he was actually murdered? Like, properly?' She saw Lena's look and added, 'Of course, you can't talk about it.'

'That's right. But I have one more question.'

'Shoot!'

'What was the Bohlens' marriage like, do you think?'

Rosa groaned. 'Well, I was expecting to be asked that, but that was before I knew it was you who'd be interrogating me.'

'Interviewing,' Lena said.

'Or that. But you must promise not to tell the boss. Please.'

Lena nodded. 'I think I can do that.'

'OK! Let me put it this way: I never understood why they got married in the first place. Not then, not now. And everything I saw later confirmed my initial feeling. They certainly were no fairy-tale couple.'

'Did they argue much?'

'Not like that. The boss – Frau Bohlen, that is – is more the type to play mind games. She goes all quiet. You can practically see it stewing in her. The atmosphere's always icy when she's like that – deepest Siberia, so to speak. If I hadn't had my own experience with Hein Bohlen, I'd have felt sorry for him.'

'Do you think Frau Bohlen has psychological problems?'

'Lena, I'm a cook, not a psychologist. But her mood swings remind me very much of my mother, who also had a difficult man at home. Sabine is very hard-working and would do anything for the kids, but you didn't ask about that.'

'Thank you for your honesty. You've helped me a great deal.'

'No problem. It's in all of our interests. I feel sick at the thought of a murderer walking around out there.'

'Don't worry, we'll get to the bottom of it. One more question. Did you notice any strangers visiting the home in the last few months?'

'Good question. The kitchen windows look out on to the back. I never saw anyone round there. As I said, since the incident with Hein, I pretty much stick to the kitchen.' She leaned her head back and breathed deeply. 'But you're right, there was someone, a man I didn't know. He didn't look like someone from social services, more like a businessman. I know the accountant and everyone at the bank. No, he must have been an outsider. If I remember it right, Hein Bohlen wasn't overly pleased to see me in the hallway. He ushered his visitor into his office and seemed annoyed when I asked if they needed coffee or anything. Does that help at all?'

'When was this, and can you describe the man?'

'About two weeks before Hein Bohlen . . . died. The man? Oh dear. Around fifty, I'd say. Dark hair, no beard, Mediterranean type, but a native German speaker, I could tell. But other than that – suits all look the same to me. White shirt, tie, dark jacket. I don't even know if I'd recognise him again.'

'Do you think your boss was afraid of him?'

'I wasn't really close enough to tell. Nervous, definitely, and as I said, he was annoyed when I showed up.'

'All right, that'll be all for now. You've been a great help – how exactly remains to be seen. Every item of information is like a piece of a puzzle and it's our job to put it together somehow. Sometimes the pieces fit and sometimes they don't.'

Rosa Behrens nodded thoughtfully. 'Shame you're here for work. Would've been good to have a cup of tea with you some time.' She grinned. 'Or some bubbly. But you're probably not allowed to meet with suspects privately, are you?'

'You're a witness, so I don't see a problem. How about you give me your number? I don't know how long I'll be on the island yet. There might be enough time.'

'Awesome! I'll put a bottle in the fridge.'

'You live on your own?'

'More or less,' Rosa replied. 'I never seem to find Mr Right. So far, no man has ever wanted the same as me. People seem to think just because you don't look half bad, men must be lining up outside your door! But what men, I ask? *My* man hasn't turned up yet. And unfortunately, you can't bake one. Not to mention the choice on our beautiful little island is rather limited . . . And what about you?'

Lena stood up. 'Let's save that story for another time. I promise I'll tell you everything when we meet up.'

'Can't wait! But catch the murderer first, please.'

◆ ◆ ◆

Lena found her colleague in the kitchen, interviewing one of the casual staff.

'Thank you,' he was saying to a short, rotund woman in her fifties. 'I have no further questions.'

The woman nodded and left the kitchen.

'I'm finished with the two casuals,' he said to Lena. 'Should we pay Frau Bohlen another visit?'

'Definitely. Did you learn anything else about the Bohlens' relationship?'

'Between the lines, yes. Sounds like there was a lot of tension.'

They found Sabine Bohlen in the office. Lena knocked at the half-open door. 'May we speak with you for a moment, please?'

'Certainly,' she said, gesturing to the chairs in front of her desk.

The two detectives sat down. 'Your husband put a very large sum of money towards the purchase of this house – eight hundred thousand euros, to be precise. We've found out that the statement concerning the source of this money was falsified.'

Sabine Bohlen stared at them in shock. 'Falsified? That simply can't be true. What are you trying to pin on my husband now?'

'Do you know anything about it?'

'No, that was well before my time. My husband told me he'd won the lottery.'

'Well, he wasn't telling the truth. The tax office will be in touch about this.' Sabine Bohlen swallowed. Lena went on. 'We spent yesterday trying to build up a picture of your husband's life. You kindly gave us a list of his friends and associates. Do you think the list is complete, or have you thought of anyone else in the meantime?'

'Of course it's complete. Why should I leave anyone out?'

'Do you know a Herbert Bergendorf?'

'Here in Norddorf?'

'One of his residences is in Nebel.'

'No, I've never heard of him. Why?'

'No particular reason. We came across his name during the course of our inquiries.' Lena unfolded the sheet of paper with the list of names and handed it to Sabine Bohlen. 'Can you think of anyone on this list who might have had something against your husband? Did he perhaps have an outstanding disagreement with anyone?'

'Possibly. It's normal for people not always to see eye to eye, but I don't know about any actual dispute.'

'From what we've learned about your husband so far, he wasn't always . . . Let's just say he wasn't the most balanced person. He lost his temper every now and then.'

'Nonsense! You can't believe everything people tell you. My husband was a very kind man. Everyone gets angry from time to time, but that's no reason to murder him.'

'Did you two fight a lot?' inquired Lena in a casual tone, as though it were hardly relevant.

Sabine Bohlen took a moment before grasping the meaning, then her face hardened. She stared at Lena as she asked, 'Who told you this nonsense?'

'Like I said, we've spent the last twenty-four hours familiarising ourselves with your husband's life, including your marital relationship. How bad were things between you?'

'I've said everything I want to say on the subject,' Sabine Bohlen hissed at Lena with an angry glare.

'There's a . . . let's call it a gap in your CV. About ten years ago, you took a year off?'

'How is that relevant?'

'Standard procedure. Were you on sick leave?'

'Even if I was, it wouldn't be any of your business. Why don't you find my husband's murderer instead of snooping around in my life?'

'Frau Bohlen,' Johann said with a warm smile, 'we have to try to get a clear picture of everyone in the victim's vicinity. We don't have a choice: it's standard procedure. When a new child arrives here at the home, I bet you're grateful for any background information you can get to help you form a more complete picture of the child.' He spoke softly and with great empathy, eventually adding, 'Were you on sick leave?'

Sabine Bohlen's attention was fixed solely on Johann now. 'Sick leave – what does that really mean? I didn't work because I was unwell. Things like that happen.'

'Were you in treatment?'

Sabine Bohlen shrugged. Then she stood up. Still looking at Johann, she muttered, 'I don't feel well. I need to lie down. Please would you come back later.'

'No problem, Frau Bohlen,' Johann said and got to his feet.

I regret nothing.

Someone had to put an end to his doings and hold him accountable.

They say vigilantes lead to social chaos, but there are exceptions. When the government is blind and can't protect its citizens, they have to do it themselves.

Now the police are here, but it'll be the same as usual. The mighty are untouchable, and if anyone gets punished, it'll be the wrong ones.

I've decided I'm no longer a victim. I'm going to fight. It's time to show the world what's been going on – what's still going on all over the country. We need the courage to stand up and act against this injustice.

It's men who commit this injustice and it's men who protect them.

It's high time something happened.

And I've started.

12

'Did we push a little too hard there?' asked Johann as Lena steered the Passat through Norddorf.

'Well, we're not bloody social workers. How many truly pleasant interviews have you sat in on? As far as I'm concerned, not many. It's our job to dig up secrets people try to hide or forget. We can never dig deep enough – especially not in this case. We've got bugger all so far, other than raising a bit of dust. And I don't have to tell you that most murder victims know their killer. We still don't even know how Hein Bohlen was killed. If it really was a rare poison, the killer must have got it from somewhere and probably has some medical knowledge.'

'Frau Bohlen doesn't strike me as someone capable of that level of premeditation,' Johann said.

'Maybe that's what she wants us to believe. In fact, is there anyone who does strike you as a likely person?' Lena pulled up in a car park outside Norddorf. 'I need some fresh air. How about a walk?'

Just up ahead lay the path along the Wadden coast. They followed it south.

'I think best when I walk,' Lena said. She told Johann what Rosa Behrens had confided in her.

'Sounds like the mysterious stranger really exists,' Johann said. 'But he could turn out to be completely harmless. We won't get far with the descriptions people have given us, in any case. The attempted rape is more interesting, though. Maybe he didn't actually give up but went ahead and raped the cook – that could be a motive.'

'Or Isabel Müller didn't tell us the whole truth and he molested her as well. What about the casual staff? Did either of them hint that Hein Bohlen might have come a little too close?'

'No, not at all. They're both aged between fifty and sixty and I'm guessing he liked them younger. But Isabel Müller would definitely fit the bill.'

Lena rolled her eyes. 'Men. We're talking about a serious offence here.'

They continued their stroll along the coastal path. A couple came towards them from the opposite direction, greeted them and walked on towards Norddorf. Lena gradually relaxed as the soothing effect of the island worked on her spirits.

'You're right,' Johann replied. 'It's serious. If Isabel Müller really was one of his victims, she knows how to hide it well, but I didn't get the impression she was keeping anything from us. And it'd be next to impossible to prove.'

'She did get a touch nervous when we asked about her relationship with her boss, but then immediately recovered. Still, let's keep it in mind. I wonder if Sabine Bohlen knew her husband had assaulted at least one of their employees? That might explain all their problems together.'

'But would it be reason enough to kill him?' asked Johann. 'Unless he violated her as well. But if the cook's telling the truth, the incident involving her took place ages ago. Why would Frau Bohlen wait so long to kill her husband? It makes no sense. And if the women knew about one another, they could have reported him together. He'd have been put away for a few years, at the very least.'

'It's not enough of a motive for me. I'd have thought a crime of passion was more likely in those circumstances – self-defence, so to speak. But our case is nothing like that.'

'What about some kind of preventative measure before he could cause any more harm: one – or all three – of the women decide to get rid of him?'

'Doesn't sound likely to me,' Lena said. 'We should ask to see the will. Sabine Bohlen told us she's the sole beneficiary, but I'd like to be sure. I can't stop thinking about the gap in her CV. The way she reacted, it could have been mental illness. If it was serious, or still is, it might have some relevance to our case. Maybe she experienced some form of violence in the past – her year out might even be connected with that. And finding out that her new husband was molesting other women might have brought all sorts of feelings of anger and disappointment to the surface. Where did she work before her year out?'

Johann pulled out his notebook. 'An orphanage near Münster. Then after the year-long gap she moved north to Oldenburg in Niedersachsen.'

'That's where Isabel Müller's brother committed suicide. Where was she working?'

'She worked as a social worker for the local authority. A straight office job, as far as I can tell.'

'So no more direct contact with people. Might have had something to do with her illness.'

Johann stopped. He cleared his throat. 'Isn't that taking it a little far? She could have had all sorts of reasons to take a year out, and even if she had a breakdown – for whatever reason – why should it have anything to do with our case? It doesn't feel right to . . . dissect the victim's wife like that.'

'She could have simply answered our question,' Lena replied.

'Most people would rather keep a mental illness secret, and for good reason. Society is extremely quick to write someone off as unstable, a loser or whatever. Look, she is in charge of a children's home, after all. I wouldn't want to go shouting it from the rooftops.'

'You have personal experience?' asked Lena.

There was a pause while Johann looked out at the Wadden Sea. At last he said, 'My mother suffered from severe depression after my sister was born. I'm ten years older than her, so I experienced it at close quarters.'

'I can imagine. But you do realise that you can't let that influence our investigation. We'll have another chat with Isabel Müller when she starts her shift this afternoon. Let's see if she gives us any clues relating to the rape theory. Anna Bauer also plays a part here. Maybe she left so abruptly because Herr Bohlen assaulted her as well.'

Johann nodded, but Lena could tell his mind was still on Frau Bohlen and his childhood memories.

'All right,' she said. 'We can't concentrate solely on the victim's immediate environment, in any case. I suggest we split up. I'll visit this Herbert Bergendorf and you go and start on Sabine Bohlen's list.'

'Visit them rather than ring?'

'Do a bit of both. Sometimes an unannounced visit is better than a phone call, but it's easier to play-act on the phone. We need to learn more about Bohlen's personality. Was he really just a touch short-tempered? What was he like around women? You decide what approach to take.'

They were on their way back to the car by now. The sun had fought its way through the clouds and covered the Wadden Sea with a warm glow. Lena stood for a moment, gazing out at the landscape of her childhood and youth, then turned abruptly and walked to the car park.

Quarter of an hour later, they pulled up outside the Bergendorf mansion. It was a new structure modelled on the old Frisian style and too large for her taste. The red-brick building with its thatched roof and white windows looked unnatural and out of place to her. Lena got out and walked up to the door. Johann waited in the car until they knew whether Herbert Bergendorf was home.

A man in his early seventies opened the door. His grey hair was neatly combed back and he wore dark trousers, a striped blue shirt, a plain tie and expensive-looking oxblood leather shoes. He looked at her expectantly.

'Herbert Bergendorf?' asked Lena, holding up her police pass.

The man stepped forward and studied it. 'CID? How interesting. How can I be of assistance to you?'

'Am I speaking with Herbert Bergendorf?'

The man smiled benevolently. 'Indeed. Did you expect someone else?'

Lena turned to Johann and gave him a nod. He started the engine and backed out.

'I'd like to ask you a few questions regarding Hein Bohlen. Your name popped up during our investigation.'

Herbert Bergendorf stepped aside and waited for Lena to enter. 'Down the hallway, second door on the right,' he said, leading the way.

Lena had watched him closely when she mentioned Bohlen's name but not even a flicker had registered on his face. The elderly man seemed completely unfazed. He neither asked what made her think that he'd known the dead man nor denied having known him.

Bergendorf led her through to his library and asked her to take a seat in one of the black leather armchairs.

'Can I get you something to drink?' he asked and sat down when Lena declined. 'How can I be of assistance to the police?'

'It's concerning the death of Hein Bohlen. Were you acquainted with him?'

'You're from the CID? I thought Hein Bohlen had died of a heart attack. On what grounds are you investigating?'

'We have reason to believe that Herr Bohlen did not die of natural causes. Were you acquainted, or even friends?'

'Not of natural causes? You mean murder?'

'Herr Bergendorf, would you please answer my question?'

For a brief moment, resistance flared up in his eyes then he raised the corners of his mouth to hint at a smile. 'Friends? No, I wouldn't call it that. We were acquainted, yes. That's all.'

'How were you connected?'

'I'm not sure if that's any business of the CID, but since you're here . . . I knew Herr Bohlen from back in Hamburg. We ran into each other here by chance one day and after that would share the occasional bottle of wine and reminisce about old times.'

'How exactly did you know each other in Hamburg?'

'We were personal acquaintances, DI Lorenzen. In my circles, it's quite normal to have a large number of associates, and one of those many people happened to be Hein Bohlen. If we passed in the street in Hamburg, we'd wish each other a good day and nothing more, but it's different on holiday here on Amrum. It's a small place, and if someone like me spends long parts of the year here, you do tend to run into one another regularly. It was good to meet someone from the old days and because of that, he and I would get together every now and then.'

'When did you last meet?'

'Good question. I don't note down personal appointments in my diary, but I'd say it was about four weeks ago.'

'Did you meet here?'

'I think so. Sometimes we would meet at the Strandhalle restaurant in Norddorf or here in Nebel, depending on the season.'

'What sort of things did you talk about?'

Herbert Bergendorf flashed his benevolent smile again. 'I honestly wouldn't remember. Small talk, I'd say. I really don't see how this is relevant.'

'Who initiated the meeting?'

Herbert Bergendorf shrugged. 'I did, perhaps. I'm not sure, really.'

'Did Herr Bohlen seem any different compared with your previous get-togethers?'

'Different? No, I would have noticed. Then again, I didn't really know him well enough to judge. But generally speaking, he was as polite and sophisticated as ever.'

'You live here on your own?'

'Basically yes, although I have many visitors – friends and former business partners.' He cleared his throat. 'But I'm guessing you mean a wife. There's no one, or rather not any more. I've been divorced for fifteen years. Are you sure I can't offer you a tea or coffee?'

'Thank you, but no, Herr Bergendorf. Getting back to your last meeting with Herr Bohlen, how long did you spend together and when exactly did you meet up?'

'One or two hours one afternoon. That's right, it must have been a Wednesday – Wednesday four weeks ago.'

'How did you organise getting together in general?'

Herbert Bergendorf scowled. 'DI Lorenzen, I may not know much about police investigations, but your questions do seem a little all over the place. What exactly is this about?' He smirked. 'Am I under suspicion? Of . . . murder?'

'Standard procedure. We're interviewing everyone who knew Hein Bohlen.'

'Standard procedure. Isn't that what detectives always say on TV? Very well, I see you're waiting for an answer. I think we tended to arrange our meetings by phone. I had his number and he had mine. It's the easiest way.'

'And where were you on the evening of the twenty-ninth of May between nine and eleven p.m.?'

Herbert Bergendorf smiled in amusement. 'Ah yes, the alibi. I know, DI Lorenzen – standard procedure. Now let's see. That was a Tuesday, if I'm not mistaken – Tuesday a fortnight ago. I can't say for certain, but I assume I was here at the house and no, I don't have witnesses. As I said, I live alone and my housekeeper isn't here at night.'

He checked his watch and stood up. 'Look, I'm sorry, but I have an appointment. If you have more questions, we'll have to continue on another occasion.'

Lena rose and shook his hand. 'Thank you for your time. One last question: how long had you known Herr Bohlen?'

Herbert Bergendorf looked irritated. 'I really don't understand how that has anything to do with your investigation.' Before Lena could reply, he continued, 'Standard procedure, yes. We've known each other for twenty years or more – I can't say exactly.'

Lena smiled. 'That's close enough. If I have any more questions, I know where to find you.'

Herbert Bergendorf walked her to the front door. 'Goodbye, Inspector. Give my regards to Chief Prosecutor Lübbers in Kiel. I'm sure you must run into him every now and again.'

Lena tried not to show her surprise, nodded at him and walked away.

13

'Oh Christ, not you again,' Leon muttered when he picked up Lena's call.

'Herbert Bergendorf,' Lena said.

'The deleted mystery email?'

'I need to find out more about him.'

'What are you after?'

'If only I knew. Just sift through his emails and anything else you can find, would you? The works. He has a house on Amrum and another in Hamburg.'

Leon hung up without saying goodbye. Lena knew this was a good sign. He'd get straight to work.

After leaving Bergendorf's mansion, Lena walked back to the main road and headed towards her aunt's house. She'd texted Johann to pick her up from there once he had finished his interviews.

On her walk over to Beke, she tried to make sense of Herbert Bergendorf's replies and demeanour. On the one hand, he'd seemed relaxed and quite normal, but she'd had the distinct impression that he'd been tense behind the blasé exterior, and very careful with his replies. He'd paused each time before speaking or repeated part of Lena's question as though gaining time in order to avoid making a mistake. It wasn't unusual for people to become nervous during an interview. They were, after all, being questioned by the police and it was a natural reaction to act as though they had something to hide. But Herbert Bergendorf was different. He'd observed her calmly, patiently, like a hunter waiting for the right moment to fire the fatal shot. Lena felt certain that she was on to something. Whether that something had anything to do with Hein Bohlen's murder remained to be seen.

Lena knocked on Beke's door. Moments later she heard footsteps in the hallway.

'Lena, what a nice surprise. I'm just preparing lunch. Are you in a rush?'

'I don't think so,' she said and checked her buzzing phone. A text from Johann. He'd be at least another hour. 'I've an hour or so.'

'Wonderful,' said Beke, hugging her niece.

Quarter of an hour later, Lena sat at the table with a plate of *Labskaus* in front of her: a dish of corned beef and potatoes with a fried egg on top.

'Yum,' said Lena. 'How did you know I was coming for lunch?'

'Because I made your favourite meal, you mean? I think it had more to do with the fact that you're on Amrum at the moment.'

'Delicious!' said Lena after she'd tried a spoonful. 'The best *Labskaus* in the whole world.'

Beke smiled and said, 'You're exaggerating, *deern.*'

After Lena had finished her second helping, she leaned back and grunted with satisfaction. 'That's exactly what I needed.'

Beke cleared the table. 'Tough day on the job?'

'We're still completely in the dark. We should have come here two weeks ago – the first forty-eight hours are crucial. Do you know a Herbert Bergendorf?'

'That peculiar bank director fellow from Hamburg?'

'He's retired, but yes, he was CEO of a large Hamburg-based bank until a few years ago.'

'Either way, I don't care much for people of his sort. He'd be better off on Sylt.'

'Sounds like he's not too popular?'

'Well, you know how long it takes for Amrum folk to accept an incomer. Generally speaking, I think it's a bit over the top myself, but in his case I understand. He seems aloof and unapproachable. My friend Gesine worked as his housekeeper for a while. He often had wealthy types visiting him from the mainland. Gesine quit after a year.'

'Do you know why?'

'Not really. She didn't want to talk about it. I think the man frightened her.' She paused. 'But don't you go running to Gesine about him now, will you?'

Lena laughed. 'Don't worry, my darling aunt, I won't. Herr Bergendorf is a witness, that's all. He knew Hein Bohlen.'

'Really? They were so very different.'

She's right, Lena thought. That's precisely what she'd thought when Bergendorf spoke of the old days in Hamburg. Beke had – as so often – hit the nail on the head.

'Yes,' she said at last.

'You could do with a strong coffee, couldn't you? At certain times, even the best cup of Amrum tea won't hit the spot – but don't you go telling anyone!' said Beke, already on her way over to the coffee machine.

Lena sighed. 'I wish you wouldn't wait on me so much.'

'Don't talk nonsense, child. You're here for once so it's my right to be able to spoil you.' The old lady poured ground coffee into the filter and switched on the machine. 'You met up with Erck?' she asked casually.

Lena chuckled. 'I didn't have a lot of choice since you kindly gave him my number.'

'He told me you'd run into each other at the beach and that he'd given you his number. He was afraid you wouldn't get in touch,' Beke said by way of apology.

'Don't worry, Beke,' Lena replied. 'He's right, though – I probably wouldn't have.'

'And?'

'And nothing! We talked about the old days, that's all, and then went home. Separately. It was good to see him. Hasn't changed much, has he?'

'Oh yes, he has! He's matured a lot. You both have. Are you going to see him again?'

Lena laughed. 'Beke, you honestly don't need to worry about my love life. Men are practically lining up on my doorstep.'

'Is that right?' asked Beke and went over to the coffee machine again, returning to the table with two steaming mugs. 'You made such a lovely couple.'

'Beke! That was such a long time ago. I made my decision and Erck couldn't and wouldn't leave Amrum. I understood him then and I still do now, but I couldn't stay. And, to be honest, I'm glad I was brave enough to take that step.'

Lena didn't mention how many times she'd regretted her decision and longed to be back on this tiny island in the North Sea. Because of Erck's decision to stay on Amrum, she'd spent the first few months following her departure in a permanent state of shock. She'd plunged into her education and training and tried to forget about him. After a terrible one-night stand with a married supervisor from her unit, she'd steered clear of men altogether for a few years. She'd realised she hadn't forgotten him entirely, however, when he appeared at the house by the beach – one very big reason she'd decided not to call him, in fact.

'And why don't I believe you, *deern?*' asked Beke thoughtfully.

'Because you've always worried about me, but I'm a big girl now and no one can hurt me any more.'

Beke sighed. 'That's what you said when you were ten, and I didn't believe you then either.'

Lena leaned forward to kiss her aunt's cheek. 'And I already loved you then as much as I do now. Don't you worry about me, I'll be fine.' Before Beke could answer, the doorbell rang. 'That'll be my colleague, come to pick me up,' Lena said, rising to her feet. 'Thank you so much for lunch. I promise I'll have more time tomorrow. I'll call you, OK?'

◆ ◆ ◆

'All good?' Lena asked as Johann tossed her the car keys.

'I spoke to five people on the phone and visited another three,' he continued as they climbed into the car. 'It's quite obvious that Bohlen was often impulsive and did not always have a grip on himself, even around his friends. I got the impression it was his wife who kept the friendships going and he was more of an appendage. I mean, no one said so outright, but it was pretty clear, reading between the lines. I'll email you the transcripts tonight, but I doubt our murderer is anyone from this lot. If there's time tomorrow I'll pay a call on the five people I spoke to on the phone.'

'You've been a busy lad.'

'Sure have,' Johann said. 'I also got hold of someone in Spain. Anna Bauer happens to be back in Germany on holiday at the moment. I've got her phone number, but no answer so far. Do you want to talk to her?'

'Yes, I do. Do you know how long she's been back and where she is?'

'She's been back for three weeks. The guy at the hotel didn't know where she's staying, though.'

'Interesting – that means she's a suspect, especially if our rape theory checks out, unless there's something else linking her to the victim. We need to find out why she quit. Could be tough over the phone, though. If we reckon there's any grounds for suspicion, one of us will have to go and visit Frau Bauer in person.'

'Tricky with just the two of us. Should we ask for back-up?'

'I don't think they'll grant us any at this stage. We need more facts and less guesswork.'

'My colleague from Oldenburg's been in touch, by the way. He took a closer look at the file regarding the suicide of Isabel Müller's brother. The investigating officers back then concluded that the reason for his depression stemmed from his childhood years and his experiences at various homes. The doctor in charge dropped a few hints in that direction without going into detail.'

'Nothing concrete?'

'Good old doctor–patient confidentiality. Losing both your parents at a young age seems reason enough to me to cause significant damage. Apparently, his sister handled it better. She works at a home now, doesn't she? She'd hardly be doing that if she was plagued by nightmares.'

'Unless she's doing it for that very reason,' Lena said. 'Let's look at these three more closely. They're an odd group, aren't they? The wife of the victim, who suffered burn-out for whatever reason at a youngish age and now pours her heart and soul into the children's home. Then there's Anna Bauer, who up and left for Mallorca out of the blue and for no apparent reason. And finally, we have Isabel Müller, whose brother may have killed himself because of traumatic experiences suffered in children's homes during his childhood, and who – formerly a troublesome child in just such a home herself – these days also works at this home for children in care. The burning question is what precise relationship each of these three women had with our victim.'

'And let's not forget about the cook. She did, after all, admit to almost having been raped by Bohlen.'

'Yes. Although I can't see why Rosa Behrens would take her revenge a whole two years later. I know she and I used to be friends and I could be biased, but even so I don't find her suspicious. She didn't need to tell us about the attempted rape. We'd never have found out.'

'Who knows? Maybe she was afraid her boss had boasted to his friends about it and one of them would tell us. If we'd heard from someone else, she'd have looked suspicious. As far as we know, Bohlen could have tried again and gone further, in which case her story would be a clever tactic.'

Lena had to admit that Johann's train of thought made sense, but still her gut feeling told her otherwise. At no point during the interview with Rosa had she got the impression that her former school friend was lying to her.

'We'll bear her in mind,' Lena said. 'I'll try Anna Bauer next. Do you have her number?'

A woman's voice answered after the fifth ring. 'Yes?'

'Am I speaking with Anna Bauer?'

'Yes.'

'My name is Detective Inspector Lena Lorenzen of CID Kiel. You'll have heard about the death of your former employer, Hein Bohlen?'

'Yes.'

'I'm investigating his death and have a few questions to ask you.' Before Anna Bauer could say 'Yes' again, Lena continued. 'How long have you been back in Germany?'

'How do I know you're really from the police? You could be—'

'I'm going to hang up and send you a photo of my police pass. If that's not enough for you, I'll give you the phone number of the CID in Kiel. You can call them and have them confirm my details. I'll call you back in a minute.'

Lena hung up and sent the photo. She waited a minute and then rang back.

'Can we talk now?' asked Lena without further ado.

'Yes.'

'So how long have you been back in Germany?'

'About three weeks.'

'Where were you on the twenty-ninth of May?'

There was a pause before Anna Bauer asked, 'Was that the Tuesday?'

'Yes, it was.' Lena could tell that the woman was trying to gain time and was interested to hear her reply.

'I think . . . yes, I think I was on Föhr, visiting a friend.'

'I need the name and address.'

'Can I text it through to you? I'll have to look it up.'

'Sure. Where are you right now?'

'In Flensburg. I'm flying back to Mallorca in a week.'

'You left the home on Amrum very suddenly. Why?'

There was another silence before Anna Bauer cleared her throat and replied, 'I wanted a change. It was always my dream to live in Mallorca.'

'But why leave so suddenly? You didn't start your new job until three months after you'd left Amrum. Were there problems at work?'

'No.'

'Frau Bauer, I'd appreciate it if you answered in a little more detail. You had no problems at work or with your boss?'

'Like I already said.' Her voice sounded annoyed, but Lena also picked up uncertainty.

'How was your relationship with Hein Bohlen?'

'Fine.'

'You were having an affair?' Lena decided not to beat about the bush, in the hope of drawing Anna Bauer out.

'Who said that?' She sounded indignant.

'We have several witness statements suggesting a love affair with Herr Bohlen.'

'That's nonsense!'

'Was it just a fling?'

'Even if – how is that any of your business?' snarled Anna Bauer.

'How long did your affair last?' Lena asked calmly.

'Not long. And it wasn't love, it was purely sex. And it's none of your business.'

'How long?'

'A year, perhaps,' Anna Bauer said after a long pause. 'It meant absolutely nothing.'

'Did you see Herr Bohlen on your recent visit?'

'No.'

'Did you only visit Föhr or did you come to Amrum too?'

'I didn't go to Amrum and I didn't see him. All right?'

'Frau Bauer, I must ask you to remain in Flensburg for the next few days. I'm sending one of our colleagues to take your statement. He'll be in touch later on today.'

'If you must,' Anna Bauer muttered.

'Yes, we must. We'll be in touch.'

Anna Bauer hung up without another word. Lena glanced at Johann, climbed out of the car and walked out of earshot before calling Ben. She quickly explained what she needed and Ben promised to take Anna's statement the following day at the latest.

'Unofficially?'

'No, you'll get an official order from Warnke, but I won't be talking to him until this evening. But you can make a start in the meantime.'

'OK!' Ben waited for more.

'I don't believe her. You'll have to put pressure on her. I need the real reason for her resignation.'

'I got it the first time, Lena.'

'Thanks again for all your help, Ben. I'd hate to ask someone I didn't know.'

Ben sighed. Clearly, he'd hoped for something more personal. 'I'll be in touch, Lena. Look after yourself.'

Lena got back in the car and told Johann she'd asked a colleague to interview Anna Bauer. 'I told him to pressure her.'

Johann raised his eyebrows but said nothing. 'Back to the home?'

'Yes, we need another word with Isabel Müller. And I've got a few more questions for her boss too.'

14

'You wanted to talk to me again?' asked Isabel Müller on greeting the two detectives.

Johann nodded. 'Is there anywhere we can talk in private?'

'The kids are all outdoors. We can sit in the dining room. I only have half an hour, though.'

'That'll be plenty,' Lena said and led the way.

Once they were all seated, Isabel Müller pulled a scrap of paper from her pocket and handed it to Johann. 'I was going to call you today in any case. One of the children has a thing for licence plates – he writes down the number of any plate he sees. I only remembered after our conversation before. I think this has to be the number of the black limousine I mentioned.'

Lena read the Hamburg licence number and raised her eyebrows. 'That's not a kid's handwriting.'

'No, of course not. I copied it from his secret book. I'd appreciate it if Jonas – that's the boy's name – didn't find out that I went through his things.'

Johann noted down the registration number and returned the scrap of paper. 'We'll check it out.'

Lena leaned forward. 'I'd like to talk some more about your relationship with Hein Bohlen. We've heard evidence that he has molested women sexually in the past. Did he ever get too close to you?'

'Molested women sexually? Who?' Isabel Müller looked at Johann and Lena expectantly. When they didn't reply, she continued, 'No, I already told you: we had a good working relationship but no contact outside of work.' She paused. 'Oh, I see – you're looking for a motive. I'm sorry, I can't help you there.'

'Could you please describe your relationship with Hein Bohlen in a little more detail?' asked Lena. 'Did you ever get the feeling he was getting closer than was strictly necessary?'

'If you mean did he ever come on to me, then no, neither verbally nor physically. He was polite but kept his distance – a normal sort of distance, I mean. We never touched apart from shaking hands. And if you mean did he ever flirt with me – no, I'd have noticed.'

'Did any of your colleagues ever mention anything to that effect?'

Isabel Müller shook her head. 'As you know, I haven't been working here long. I've never met my predecessor or spoken with her. I'm on good terms with my other colleagues but they're all locals. I think it takes a while before people here . . .' She broke off. 'And things are pretty chaotic on the island right now. No wonder, with you people here looking for a murderer. Folk are frightened.'

'You were in a home yourself as a child?' Lena's question came out of the blue.

Isabel Müller seemed thrown for a moment but recovered quickly. 'Yes, I was in a home for a while as a child.'

'With your younger brother?'

Isabel Müller stiffened, then she glared at Lena. 'Leave Florian out of it!'

'I'm sorry, Frau Müller, but this is a murder investigation and we need to look at everything. How was your relationship with your brother?'

'That's personal,' she said, calm again. 'He never came to Amrum and had nothing to do with Herr Bohlen. I refuse to talk about him. You know very well that he took his own life.'

'Yes, we know. You and your brother were close?'

'Yes, of course.' She rose. 'I have work to do. Is there anything else?'

'Not for now,' Lena said. 'Is Frau Bohlen available?'

◆ ◆ ◆

Two minutes later, Johann knocked at the door of Sabine Bohlen's office. She called them in.

She gave them a tired smile. 'What else can I do for you? I thought you had finished with the interviews.'

Lena and her young colleague seated themselves in front of her desk.

'Thank you for taking the time to talk to us again. New facts are emerging all the time, and we'll keep coming back until the case is solved.'

Frau Bohlen put down her pen. 'I understand, but . . .' She didn't finish the sentence.

'We've been talking to Anna Bauer. She's been working on Mallorca for a while but is currently on leave in Germany. Have you seen Frau Bauer on Amrum during the last three weeks?'

'No, of course I haven't. I'd have told you.'

'Why? We never asked you,' Lena asked quickly, so as not to give Frau Bohlen much time to think. 'Why would you have told us?'

Flustered, Sabine Bohlen looked down at her hands. 'I guess because it would have been important, wouldn't it?'

'Yes, it would have. You knew Frau Bauer was having an affair with your husband?'

Sabine Bohlen swallowed. 'An affair? What are you talking about?'

'You heard me. They had a secret relationship. Did you know?'

'Nonsense – a relationship! Do you even know what that means? You're talking about sex – meaningless physical interactions. You can't call that a relationship!'

'You knew they were having sex?' asked Lena.

'I wouldn't put it past that little bitch.' Her voice sounded tense and her hands trembled slightly. She stared into the distance, her cheeks flushed.

Johann cleared his throat. 'I know what you mean, Frau Bohlen. We merely wondered if this – let's call it a fling – was known to anyone else?'

'How should I know?' muttered Sabine Bohlen. 'He never told me.'

'But you suspected it?' asked Johann cautiously.

Sabine Bohlen gave a resigned shrug.

Lena leaned forward. 'I'm afraid I can't spare you from hearing what else we found out in the course of our investigation so far. Your husband molested at least one other woman – attempted rape, you could even call it.'

Sabine Bohlen stared at Lena in shock. 'What on earth? That's an outrageous accusation! My husband would never have done anything like that. It's an outright lie! I'll sue you if you spread this any further.' She stumbled to her feet, knocking her chair to the ground. 'I want you to leave this minute.'

Lena stood up. 'Please calm yourself. We're leaving for now, but we'll have to continue this conversation tomorrow.'

Johann held out his hand to the woman. 'Goodbye, Frau Bohlen.'

She automatically reached for Johann's hand but said nothing. The two detectives left the office and returned to their car.

Lena snapped at Johann when she noticed his look. 'Yes, that was necessary. We can't give her any special kid-glove treatment – she's as much under suspicion as the rest of them.'

Johann shrugged and said, 'I still don't have to like it, do I?'

Lena rolled her eyes and muttered, 'Sensitive little flower . . .'

They drove back to the house in silence. Johann retreated to his room to work on his report, while Lena sat down at the kitchen table to search the Internet for the phone details of Isabel Müller's last employer.

After being transferred twice, she finally had Isabel's former line manager from children's social services on the phone.

'To whom am I speaking?' asked a calm voice.

'Good afternoon. This is Frau Rosenbach from the German Pension Fund, North. I'm looking at the file of Frau Isabel Müller, who worked for you up until six months ago.'

'Yes? And how may I help?'

'I don't have any new contact details for Frau Müller. Something must have gone wrong at our end when she switched jobs. But she definitely no longer works for you, is that right?'

The woman at the other end of the line gave a dry laugh. 'No, that's quite correct. Frau Müller left us all of a sudden – at least, she handed in her resignation. As for where she went next, I can't tell you, I'm afraid.'

'That must be why we're missing some data – because she left so suddenly. Young people are always in such a rush, aren't they?'

' "In a rush" is putting it mildly. Her resignation came out of nowhere. She was there when I went on holiday and gone when I came back. I was given no time to find a replacement – not much fun, I can tell you. Never mind, you don't want to hear all that. I'm sorry I can't be of help. Would you like me to put you through to Personnel? They might be able to tell you more.'

'Yes, please.'

When the next voice answered, Lena apologised and said she had the wrong number.

The next call was to the Münster branch of the Pension Insurance Fund. Lena claimed she had worked for a health insurance company.

'Good afternoon. I'm sorry to bother you with this, but I don't know what else to do. I'm calling about Sabine Bohlen, née Lauer. I'm missing some documentation from 2005, from the clinic Frau Bohlen was attending. It cropped up during an internal audit and I got the short straw. Is there any chance you might have a copy of the documents in your own files?'

'Frau . . . ?'

'Hansen. Hannah Hansen.' She gave an embarrassed laugh. 'My father had a thing for matching first and last names.'

'Frau Hansen, you know very well we can't give out any information over the phone. Data protection laws and all that.'

'Of course, Herr Block. I've already been instructed about our data protection laws about five times today. I'm really just after a very small hint as to which clinic I'm supposed to be looking for and then I can fix the problem myself.'

'Then I'd suggest you ask your client. She should be able to tell you right away.'

'I'd love to, but she was involved in an accident and is lying in a coma – that's why I got her file out in the first place. Her husband was no help, and to be honest, I don't want to bother him with a petty matter. He's got enough on his plate right now.'

The man on the phone groaned theatrically. 'You know perfectly well I'm not allowed to—'

'Oh, please, Herr Block!' begged Lena. 'I'd truly—'

'Hang on, I'll go and check.'

Two minutes later, Lena had the name of the clinic and was thanking Herr Block profusely.

Next, she called Leon. He picked up with his usual lack of greeting.

'You all right?' asked Lena.

'So far.'

'Sorry to bother you again. How did you get on with Herbert Bergendorf?'

'Working on it. His computer is extremely clean.'

'Extremely? But you still found something?'

'Working on it, like I said. You do realise it's not that easy to hack someone's computer?'

Lena knew that hacking into a personal computer depended on a great deal of luck. A Trojan horse was sent to the intended victim via email and the user then had to open the email for it to take effect. Only then would Leon have a chance of accessing the hard drive.

'I really appreciate what you're doing for me, Leon. Honestly. I'm sorry I'm so pushy at the moment. It's just that time's running out and I've got virtually nothing.'

'All right, stop rabbiting on. I'm in. Believe it or not, the posh gentleman's got Tor on his laptop.'

Lena knew he was talking about the free computer software enabling the user to browse the Internet anonymously, as well as access the Dark Web.

'Well, what do you know – Herr Bergendorf's on the Dark Web. Who'd have thought?'

'Means I can't trace what he's been up to. But I've got my eye on him now. I'll see when he logs on and then we'll know a bit more. I reckon he's got something going on. And before you ask – yes, I want to find out. Like I told you, I'm in. But you'll just have to wait.'

Lena hadn't heard this many sentences in a row from Leon in a long time. Clearly, he viewed Bergendorf's squeaky-clean laptop as a personal challenge.

'Next time he logs on, I'll get the data sent through automatically and then we'll see.'

'Thanks, Leon. That sounds great. Just one more thing.'

Leon said nothing. At first Lena thought he'd hung up, but then she heard him groan with annoyance. She told him the name of the clinic Johann's colleague from Oldenburg had given them – the clinic Florian Müller had been treated in – and asked him to look for his patient file.

'That'll take a while – two, three days. Will you still need it by then?'

'Yes, it might be important.'

'Let's hope so,' he said and hung up.

Lena shut her laptop down and walked over to Johann's door. She knocked and he asked her to come in.

'I found out a few more things,' Lena said.

Johann listened attentively while she told him about Isabel Müller's sudden change of job and Sabine Bohlen's stay at a psychiatric hospital.

'You do realise we can't use any of this in court?' It was clear from Johann's tone that he disapproved of Lena's methods.

'We don't have all the time in the world and we don't have a back-up team to help us look at every detail. Sometimes you just have to think outside the box a little.'

'Sure, but if we can't use the information in the end because it was obtained illegally, then it's not much use, is it?'

'Just you wait and see!' said Lena. 'I'm going to report back to Kiel and then knock off for the night. You should do the same.'

DSU Warnke sounded pleased to hear from her. 'How did you get on?'

'Well, we've put the cat among the pigeons and are waiting to see what comes out.' She summarised their day without giving away all the details. She also asked Warnke to issue an official order for Ben's interview with Anna Bauer. There was no news from the Institute for Tropical Medicine in Hamburg. Finally, she asked, 'I urgently need the phone data. Any progress with that at your end?'

'We've had a few issues with that. Tomorrow, hopefully.'

In all the time she'd known Warnke, she'd never heard him speak of issues. He was the kind of man who made things happen, and fast.

'Chief Prosecutor Lübbers?' asked Lena on a hunch.

DSU Warnke said nothing. That was new too. Eventually, he said, 'Like I said, tomorrow.'

'I understand,' Lena said, not entirely sure what to make of it. 'Anything else I should know?'

'Look after yourself,' Warnke replied and hung up.

'What the hell was that about?' muttered Lena, dropping the phone on her bed.

There it was again, that strange feeling she'd had after her very first conversation with Warnke before this all kicked off. She thought once again that there had to be more to the case than just manslaughter or murder. She lay down and stretched out her legs, running through her interview with Herbert Bergendorf in her mind. She'd rarely dealt with anyone so slippery. He'd had his facial expressions and body language under perfect control the entire time and even now Lena was struggling to see how he might fit with all the other pieces of this puzzle. Usually, she liked to let her impressions of an interview or conversation sink in for a few hours before thinking it over again. Her overriding disadvantage had been the fact that she had nothing incriminating whatsoever against Herbert Bergendorf other than the not fully deleted email Leon had acquired illicitly. Really, Bergendorf could have shut the door in her face with a frosty smile. Why hadn't he? Had he wanted to see how much his enemies knew? Did he want to meet her so he could gauge her strength? Or was she just setting out on a wild-goose chase with him? Luckily, Leon had managed to hack into his computer in record time, and now everything depended on the results of Leon's spy program. Even so, Lena would need Bergendorf to make mistakes she could prove through legitimate means.

She picked up her phone and called Enno Eilts. 'May I bother you again?' she asked after the preliminary greetings.

'Of course you may, Lena. Any news?'

Lena gave another report of the day's events but this time did not hold anything back. She'd told Enno about Leon long ago.

'I hope your golden boy won't be your downfall one day,' he said with concern. 'I won't be able to bail you out.'

'I know, Enno, but I don't see any other way right now. What can you tell me about Chief Prosecutor Lübbers? I've never had much to do with him.'

'He's fierce and clever, and someone to steer clear of. He's about to move up a rank and take over from old Berger. I never could stand Lübbers, don't ask me why. Thankfully, I never had much to do with him either. Why ask?'

'Bergendorf mentioned him in a strange comment. I rather think it was offered as a threat.'

'Those two would suit each other perfectly – just the kind of person Lübbers likes to surround himself with: the rich or the beautiful. Please, Lena, look after yourself!'

She sighed. 'You have no idea how many times I've heard that lately.'

'I'm serious. By the way, my own research finally bore some fruit. Warnke used to be stationed in Brandenburg – I'm sure you knew that already. I've since talked with a former colleague over there who said Warnke had a terrific detection rate – hardly anything left unsolved, in fact. Apparently, he was obsessed with one particular case, though, according to my colleague, concerning an investigation into an international child-trafficking ring spanning right across Europe. In the end, Warnke was forced to close the case as it was taking too long, was costing too much and there was too little chance of a successful outcome. You know the game we're in. With all that in mind, the way he treated you during the investigation into that little boy's disappearance is beginning to make sense. He's quite clearly got a bee in his bonnet about paedophiles as far as missing children are concerned – no looking at other possibilities, just doggedly following that one scenario.'

'You think my case could have something to do with this?' asked Lena, puzzled.

'I'm too far away from the facts to be able to say anything for certain, but you are investigating in and around a children's residential home. It wouldn't be the first time those monsters were targeting an institution of that nature.'

'The victim's wife is a professional caregiver and educator and would do anything to protect her children. She'd never agree to anything like that.'

'Are you absolutely certain? I know you can normally rely on your gut feeling, Lena, but I've interviewed people I could swear wouldn't hurt a fly, and then it turns out they were the driving force behind the most unimaginable cruelties.'

'I know what you mean. I'll bear that in mind.'

Lena heard a noise outside and a moment later someone knocked on her window. She turned to see Erck, laughing, holding up a key.

I feel sick when I think about it.

Why did I close my eyes to this terrible wrong for so long? It was so obvious and yet I just didn't see. I blame myself endlessly but I can't turn back time, no matter how badly I want to.

That detective woman is clever. She won't give up in a hurry. That's why I need to act now. I'm running out of time. But I've made my decision: I'm going to carry on. I have to, or everything so far would have been for nothing.

But I need to be careful. More careful than with him. He was such an easy target, that stupid, arrogant sap of a man.

The time for reckoning has come.

15

'Erck, you know very well—'

'Shush! How many times did we use to say we'd like to watch the sunset from the lighthouse? Who knows when you'll be back next? Right, I'll wait in the car. Bring a jacket – it might get a little chilly later.' Erck turned and walked back along the narrow cobblestone path to his car.

Lena closed the window. Erck was right. The two of them used to fantasise about getting into the Amrum lighthouse at night. She assumed the key in Erck's hand was for the lighthouse door – he must have borrowed it from his mate who ran guided tours in the mornings. Hadn't she wanted to switch off from work in any case, so she could tackle the next day with renewed energy? Lena grabbed her jacket, called out to Johann and left the house.

'I hope I didn't drag you away from your work,' said Erck, steering his old Golf back on to the main road towards Norddorf.

Lena laughed. 'You're still a terrible liar. Of course you wanted to drag me away from work – that was your plan all along.'

Erck pretended to look guilty. 'I'll take you back in two hours and then you can chase after your criminals for the rest of the night, OK?'

'They're not my personal criminals – they affect everyone in society, but enough of that. I'll take the evening off. I only hope you've got the right key.'

'Hey, what do you think I am? I've planned everything to perfection. I've been making schemes for your abduction since last night.'

Lena smirked. 'You're a little bit nuts, you do know that? Better focus on the road . . .'

'Ha, you haven't changed much either.'

They'd left Norddorf and were now on the open road towards Nebel.

'I'm not the same Lena,' she said quietly.

'Says who?'

'We were practically children, Erck. We're pretty grown-up now.'

Erck slowed as they approached Nebel. 'So you've suddenly become a whole different person at thirty? OK then, how are you planning to be at forty – old and bitter? Let alone at fifty . . . Lena, we're young still! We've got our whole lives ahead of us.'

Lena's gaze slid across the thatched roofs as they drove along. She felt an intense longing to turn back time several years. Would she have decided differently? Would she have stayed if she'd known what her life would be like today?

'Promise me something?' asked Erck in a serious tone.

When Lena didn't reply, he continued, 'Just for tonight, let's forget the last fourteen years ever happened. I've imagined us two up there so many times that I started believing we'd actually done it. I need closure, and I'm guessing you do too.'

'Maybe,' Lena whispered.

Erck sped up. They sat in silence as he took a sharp right on to a gravel road and then, after bumping along it for a little way, he pulled up at a small car park. He reached behind him and lifted a bag from the back seat. 'You coming?'

Slowly, they climbed the steps to the bottom of the lighthouse. When they reached the red and white tower, Erck unlocked the door and stepped aside. She could hear the smile in his voice as they picked their way up the winding staircase. 'Do you remember how many steps there are?'

'One hundred and seventy-two,' Lena said.

'And do you know how many times I've come up here in the last fourteen years?'

'Tell me.'

'Not once. I've been waiting for you.'

Lena stopped. 'Erck . . .'

'That wasn't a declaration of love,' he said. 'I just couldn't do it. Crazy, isn't it? Another reason why I needed to do this with you right now.'

'Didn't you say before to forget the last fourteen years?'

Erck nodded, grasped Lena's hand and pulled her along. 'Did I mention that the view's going to be spectacular this evening?'

'No, you didn't.'

He checked the time. 'Sunset's in half an hour. Come on, let's go!'

A metal stairway replaced the stone steps for the last section. A cool breeze welcomed them when Erck opened the door on to the platform. Lena walked over to the railing. The impact of the view took her breath away, transporting her fourteen years back in time in an instant. She felt her eyes well up and tried to blink away the tears. The huge fireball of the setting sun sank into the sea, tinting the horizon with a bright orange-yellow.

From the corner of her eye she watched Erck, who gazed at the spectacle in fascination. 'Incredibly beautiful,' he muttered.

'Yes,' Lena said. 'I'd always wanted to see this view at sunset.'

He bent down and took something from his bag, then handed Lena a champagne flute. 'Great – they didn't break.' He popped the cork of a bottle of champagne, filled both their glasses and, raising his, said, 'This was part of my dream.' Their eyes met. 'To dreams!'

Lena clinked glasses with him and took a sip before turning back to the stunning view. In silence they watched the sun disappear into a glowing red sea.

'What else was in your dream?' asked Lena without taking her eyes off the horizon.

'Something about a ring. I don't really remember now.'

She turned to him. He was very close. 'I don't want to hurt you a second time, Erck,' Lena whispered.

'You won't,' he whispered back and kissed her softly on the mouth. After a moment's hesitation, she returned the kiss.

For a while they just stood there, holding each other tightly.

'The minutes up here with you were more beautiful than all my dreams combined,' Erck said softly. 'Thank you for coming.'

'Thank you for bringing me.'

There was a silence and then Erck asked, 'Will you come back to mine?'

When Lena nodded, Erck sealed the bottle of champagne, wrapped a towel around the glasses and put everything back into the bag. He looked at Lena. 'You sure?'

Lena held out her hand and smiled.

◆ ◆ ◆

'Good morning,' Lena said and grinned into the kitchen. 'I'll have a quick shower and then we can get started.'

'Morning,' replied Johann with a twinkle in his eye. 'I was about to call the police and report you missing.'

'I doubt Sergeant Reimers would have got out of bed for me.'

'Who knows . . . ? Maybe we've got him completely wrong.'

'Yeah, maybe,' Lena muttered and disappeared into the bathroom.

When she'd woken in Erck's arms earlier that morning, he'd smiled at her and asked how she had slept. She'd kissed him and curled more tightly into the warmth of his body.

Lena braced her arms against the walls of the shower cubicle as the hot water coursed down her body. She replayed last night in her mind and asked herself if staying at Erck's had been the right thing to do. It had felt like coming home. Would she hurt Erck again? No, he was a grown man and knew what he was doing. Their night together had just felt right to Lena. Everything would fall into place. Lena turned off the water and climbed out of the shower.

'Right, let's get a little order into this mess,' Lena said, sipping the coffee Johann handed her. 'Motive, means, opportunity. First of all, we have the wife. Her husband not only cheated on her but molested at least one of their employees – when they'd hardly been married two minutes as well. Not what I'd call a happy marriage. The children's home has become the centre of her universe. No doubt she'd have lost it if they had divorced. Since we still don't know how Hein Bohlen died, we can't even speculate about how she might have done it. If it was indeed an unknown poison, we've no clue as to how Sabine Bohlen might have obtained it. She has no alibi for his time of death. She's emotionally unstable and spent time in a psychiatric hospital. However, the fact that she was doubtful it was a heart attack right from the offset does speak in her favour.'

'I doubt she's capable of planning murder and seeing it through. In the heat of the moment, maybe, but that's hardly the case here,' said Johann.

'She did have a strong motive, though, and she was very close to the victim – she only needed to wait for the right opportunity – and like I said, there's no alibi. What I'd really like to know is if she knew about his affair and the attempted rape. I'll talk to Rosa again.' Lena suppressed a yawn. She'd not had more than four hours' sleep the previous night. 'By the way, have you noticed that Sabine Bohlen hasn't asked us when we're going to release her husband's body? Usually, it's the first thing relatives want to know.'

Johann nodded. 'You're right.'

'It's been two weeks already. But OK, fine, maybe she's still in shock and can't think straight.'

'The funeral director didn't think so,' Johann said pensively. 'And listening to her talk, she's really only interested in the children's home. How and why her husband was killed doesn't seem to bother her too much.'

'All right, next on the list is Isabel Müller. At first she seemed beyond suspicion because of the short time she's been at the home. But having heard the statements of Rosa Behrens and Anna Bauer, I think it's more than likely that Hein Bohlen tried it on with her too. Frau Müller has denied this from the start, but she could be trying to protect herself – after all, Bohlen lost his colleague with benefits when Anna Bauer upped and left. I found a photo of Frau Bauer online and I'd say her successor is a similar type. I really do think it's highly likely that Hein Bohlen tried it on with her as well – another thing to ask Rosa about. More significant, in my opinion, is her lying about being unemployed when she heard about the position here, when it was quite the opposite. I can't figure it out. Did she want to work here at all costs, or does she have some other tie to Amrum and just happened to hear about the position? She knew she couldn't muck around: the home needed a new carer straight away. Do we know if the job was even advertised?'

Johann opened his notebook and leafed through the pages. 'No, but that shouldn't be hard to find out.'

'So far, we don't really have a motive for Frau Müller. Of course, Bohlen might have molested or even raped her, but would you then go and plan out such a strangely meticulous murder? I reckon an act of passion would be far more likely. I think Frau Müller is more the type to plan her approach, though. No alibi, just like Sabine Bohlen. We have no idea if she might have access to dangerous poisons. I really hope we find out why Anna Bauer quit so suddenly because it might just tell us a little more about Isabel Müller too. I somehow think the two resignations are linked.' Lena could tell Johann was holding back a question. She guessed he was trying to work out who her contact was at Flensburg. 'Well, I'm hoping we'll know more by lunchtime. Who else have we got?'

'The cook,' Johann said. 'She was the victim of sexual harassment, albeit quite a while ago, it seems – though we can only take Frau Behrens' word for that. Why shouldn't Hein Bohlen have tried again? What if he kept trying until he succeeded? That would definitely be a motive. Personally, I thought it was odd from the start that she claims never to have told anyone about the incident. She's a cook – she'd have found a new job in no time. But instead, she's supposed to have carried on as if nothing happened?'

'Why do you think she told us then?'

'Fear of being found out: better to give away a small part of the truth than to be caught with a big fat lie. She may very well have a motive. She'd have had ample opportunity, and we don't know the means for any of them. To me, she's just as much a suspect as the other three.'

'Which leads me on to the fourth woman: Anna Bauer. Right from the outset, her sudden disappearance rang alarm bells with me. But back then we thought she was in Spain and out of the question, and now we know she was on Föhr – different story.'

'But then she would've had to spend the night on Amrum. There's no ferry late at night and she couldn't have walked.'

'Actually, she might have, at low tide,' Lena said and went to fetch the tide chart from the wall. 'Bingo!'

'In the middle of the night? How long would that take?'

'You could easily do it in three hours – less if you know your way around. But that's just it. Anna Bauer would basically have to be a trained Wadden guide to do the trip at night.'

'Shouldn't be hard to find out,' Johann said, picking up his phone to call the children's home. He gave a short whistle when he hung up. 'She took the children out on regular hikes around the Wadden and completed a special training course.'

'Well, look at that – not such a crazy idea after all then, though staying the night would have been so much easier. It would be utter madness to try crossing the Wadden in the dark, but then murder's a fit of insanity as well. So we can't cross her off the list until we know whether or not she was on the island that evening.'

'I've emailed you the interviews with the casual staff. I don't see anything suspicious there at all.'

'I'll take a look later. Let's assume for now that the two casuals are out of the picture. Now what about the wider circle of contacts? The accountant seems only to have a professional interest in the home and in Bohlen. He was reasonably fast in cooperating, even though he could have refused. The funeral director had nothing to do with Bohlen until he was dead. The GP had no relations with Herr Bohlen outside of his practice either.'

'Although he's the only one so far who might be able to get his hands on poison,' Johann suggested. 'But then, what would his motive be?'

'Is he married?'

Johann grinned. 'You could say so. He's in a civil partnership with another man – just in case you thought he might be interested in Sabine Bohlen.'

'Yes, I had wondered – clutching at straws right now, I guess. Never mind. Right, next we have our colleague Reimers, who can't explain those missing twenty minutes, and finally, the list of friends and associates. Anything useful there?' When she noticed Johann's look, she added quickly, 'I know, I was supposed to read your report.'

'Yes, you were, but no, there's nothing. Like I said, I was going to visit five of them in person today, but I've already spoken with them on the phone. Still, it won't hurt to see them face to face.'

'The eight hundred thousand and the large cash withdrawals bother me. The money's most likely dodgy and practically untraceable now. If Hein Bohlen wasn't a gambler, then he may have been blackmailed – not unthinkable in view of what we know of his character. Perhaps one of the women has evidence of being raped by him and was blackmailing him, although we've found no evidence to that effect. On balance, I think it's more likely the withdrawals were late repayments for the original loan.'

'Tricky. There must be some other leads we can chase up on that.'

'Great – and then we have Herr Bergendorf and his massive mansion.'

Johann raised his eyebrows. 'That's not a crime, as far as I know.'

'DS Grasmann, honestly, you should have become a lawyer or a judge. No, being wealthy in itself is not a crime, but—'

'Wait and see,' Johann said, finishing her sentence for her.

Lena grinned. 'At last!'

16

'Ben, hi!' Lena had just picked up her phone. 'What have you got for me?'

'How are you?' he asked in return. Ben knew about Lena's history with the island.

'Good. I'm doing fine.'

'Glad to hear it. Can't be easy, after all those years?'

'Well, do you have anything for me?' she asked impatiently.

'I think so. I visited Frau Bauer and tried to interview her. When she wouldn't talk, I took her over to the station. Interrogation room, nice and dark, you know the deal. After an hour we finally started getting somewhere. I've sent you the link – listen to the recording if you get the time. I also emailed you a list of time stamps for the important bits.'

'Can you fill me in?'

'Course. That's why I called.' He sighed. 'Among other reasons. All right, I focussed on three points: the abrupt resignation, the affair with her boss, and her alibi for the night of the murder. To put it in a nutshell, she admitted that her successor . . .'

He paused. Lena guessed he was searching his documents for a name.

'. . . Yes, this is it. Isabel Müller got in touch and persuaded her to give up her job. It took a while before she admitted that any money had changed hands – she wouldn't say how much, though – and I can only guess as to whether Frau Müller found other ways to put on the pressure too.' He paused again. 'She'd already admitted to her affair with Herr Bohlen on the phone to you. To me, it sounded like things weren't always smooth sailing between the two of them. She wanted him to leave his wife; he wanted sex with no strings attached. She hinted that Herr Bohlen could turn rather forceful to get what he wanted – but I couldn't get to the bottom of quite what that meant exactly. She seemed to realise all of a sudden that she was landing herself with a motive. She backtracked at that point and said she hadn't meant it the way it sounded. All in all, I'd say she was glad to be rid of him. Her new job on Mallorca sounds like her dream come true – her eyes literally lit up when she talked about it. And she's shit-scared we might cancel her flight and force her to stay put. I told her that's your decision and she'd better tell us the truth. Right, as to her alibi . . . She said she spent the whole evening with a friend. I guess you're still checking it out, but it sounded real enough to me. She bitched about Isabel Müller at least three times, blaming her for everything.'

'What was your impression? Do you reckon she could have done it?'

'I kept asking myself the same thing. Every now and then I had the feeling she was play-acting, but the next minute she'd sound completely genuine. I couldn't vouch for her, though. If her friend confirms her alibi, she's in the clear for now, in any case – unless they're particularly close friends. Föhr isn't far from your crime scene, is it? I guess you'll be questioning her yourself.'

'Definitely.' Lena told Ben about their speculation that Anna Bauer could have walked back over to Föhr at low tide.

'No way!' Ben said. 'Listen, I don't know much about the case, but if you think you might be on to something, good luck with proving it.'

'Back to the original and right now most important point: Isabel Müller paid her to quit her job?'

'Yep, though she didn't put it that way. Compensation, she called it, although that would usually be paid by your employer, not your successor. Like I said, I think there might have been something else behind all this. Do you think Frau Müller could have known that Anna Bauer was sleeping with Bohlen?'

'I doubt it. Unless she had the home under surveillance – but even then it would have taken a huge bit of luck to catch them in the act. I think we can safely assume she didn't know. Did Anna Bauer say anything as to why Isabel Müller was so keen on the job?'

'I kept asking precisely that but she wouldn't give me a straight answer. Either she doesn't know or she won't say. Personally, I think it's the former, but there's no guarantee.'

'Great work, Ben, and thank you so much. Perfect timing as well. We'll head straight to the home now and ask Isabel Müller a few more questions.'

'No trouble at all. And how's our boy doing? I bet he's head over heels in love with you by now.'

Lena laughed. 'Do I detect jealousy? Don't you fret – he's not making eyes at me yet. I'm not even sure he's into women.'

'Is that right? I hadn't noticed. Grasmann keeps himself to himself.' Ben paused. 'And yes, of course I'd be jealous. What did you think?'

'Drop it, Ben. But thanks again for all your help. Did you make it clear to Frau Bauer that she's not to leave the country before my say-so?'

'I just told you.'

'I'm sorry. You did. Thank you for acting so quickly. I'll be in touch when we've found out some more.'

'Lena?'

'Yes?' she replied. Would there be another *Look after yourself*?

'My marriage . . .' Ben took a deep breath. 'I tried, honestly, but it's finished. As much as I wish it were otherwise.'

Lena swallowed. This was the last thing she'd been expecting. 'I'm so sorry to hear that, Ben, really I am.'

'I just wanted you to hear it from me first. It's got nothing to do with you, or only very little. Even couples therapy didn't help.' His voice sounded low and broken. 'Yep, that's how it is, sadly.'

'You're still living together?'

'Yes, we're trying. For the little ones' sake. I don't know how long we can keep it up.' He groaned. 'You've got to go, I know. Maybe we can talk sometime after the case. What do you think?'

'Yes, sure.'

'See you, Lena.'

'Look after yourself, Ben.'

Lena stared down at her phone display for a while. Why hadn't she noticed Ben was miserable in their earlier conversations? Had she been focussed so entirely on herself and the case, or had she simply not wanted to know? Joe, Erck and now Ben – what a mess.

And would Erck now have expectations she couldn't meet either? Their night together had felt good and right and Lena didn't regret a second of it. She'd once read somewhere that a woman's first big love played a significant role throughout her life. She had never properly said goodbye to Erck – was that what last night had been about? She couldn't tell. She wanted to hold on to the happy feeling for as long as possible and not worry about the future just yet. And Ben? She just didn't have the heart to tell him over the phone that he'd only ever been a one-night stand to her. The right man at the right time. Nothing more, nothing less. She'd need to have a proper conversation with him as soon as she was free.

Johann knocked at the door. 'Ready to go?'

'Just a minute!' Lena called out and got up to arrange her hair and put on a touch of make-up in front of the mirror.

On the way to the children's home, Lena told Johann what she'd learned about Isabel Müller and Anna Bauer.

'Quite the creative job search,' Johann said. 'I can't wait to hear her explanation. Which one of us goes to Föhr to interview the friend?'

'Let's decide on that later,' Lena said as they pulled up at the home. 'I'd like to speak with Rosa Behrens first.'

'On your own, I'm guessing?'

'Probably best, I think.'

'You're the boss,' Johann muttered, holding open the front door for her.

A short while later, Lena was watching her former school friend as she prepared lunch in the kitchen.

'You still have a few questions for me, Lena?'

The DI nodded. 'Unlike me, my colleague's not one hundred per cent convinced you're telling the truth regarding the harassment from your employer.'

Rosa Behrens looked up with amusement. 'Men!'

'He finds it hard to believe Bohlen would have left you alone after just one attempt.'

'I think your colleague's trying to find a likely motive for me,' Rosa said with a grin. 'I'm sorry, but it really was just the one time.'

'Why didn't you report him?'

'And then what? You know how ruthless the gossip factory can be on this beautiful island of ours. I didn't want to risk ending up unemployed. It would have been my word against his. I'd have lost my job because of bad blood with the boss, and nothing at all would have happened to him. I'm right, aren't I?'

Lena knew Rosa had a point. Even though public awareness of sexual harassment in the workplace had grown significantly in recent times, the victim still had to face the torment of a court case, with no idea what the outcome might be – if it even came to that.

'So you chose a different route?' asked Lena.

'So to speak. I told him crystal clear what to expect if he so much as looked at me again. Trust me – I was so angry, he believed every word I said. We had a deal: I wouldn't tell and he'd leave me alone.'

'And you're absolutely certain that no one in the home knew what had happened?'

'Absolutely certain? Well, I guess you can never be totally sure. You never can tell quite what's going on with Sabine, for instance. And Anna? I don't think so. I really don't think the casual staff know anything, and I don't reckon the children would notice something like that.'

'Did you know that Anna Bauer and Herr Bohlen were having an affair?'

'Let's just say she didn't tell me. I had a vague idea, but I really couldn't care less what the two of them got up to. Is that why she ran off like that?'

'I can't tell you. How would you rate Isabel Müller's relationship with Hein Bohlen?'

'You mean, would she also have been . . . ? She'd definitely have been his type, and Isabel does like to act all mysterious. Sometimes the two of them did seem very close. But to me it just looked like Isabel wanted to suck up to the boss – God knows why. Would she go so far as to shag him, though . . . ? I've really no idea.'

'Do you think Frau Bohlen knew of his affair with Anna Bauer?'

'Maybe she had a suspicion, like I did, but maybe she wasn't really bothered one way or the other either.'

'She'd do just about anything to protect the home, wouldn't she?'

Rosa pondered the question a while. 'Aren't all women like that, though? Ready to fight tooth and nail to protect the ones we love?'

Lena smiled. 'Thank you for being so open with me, Rosa. I won't keep you any longer or the kids'll go hungry today.'

Rosa grinned. 'Don't you worry, my love, I've never let anyone go hungry. As for you—'

'I know,' said Lena, 'I'll look after myself. Thanks.'

'That's right. Hey, I'm allowed to say that – remember how I used to protect you from those nasty boys in the other class?'

'I remember – even though I was usually more the daredevil out of the two of us.' Lena tapped the gun on her belt. 'These days I can look after myself.'

Rosa leaned over and gave her a peck on the cheek. 'I'm so glad you're in charge of the investigation and not some bloke who'd have arrested me long ago.'

Lena left the kitchen and found Johann playing a board game with two boys in the common room.

'Max and Jakob have the day off from school and invited me to join them,' he said. Looking at the boys, he added, 'Sorry, lads, I need to get on with some work now, but I reckon I'd have lost anyway.'

The children beamed and proudly shook Johann's hand in farewell.

'I hope you weren't interviewing those kids?' Lena asked, once they were out in the corridor.

'Not really. Or should I say, "Wait and see"?'

Lena smirked. 'Ready to brave the lioness in her den?' She knocked at the office door and entered.

Sabine Bohlen was sitting at her desk, looking through some files. 'You again! I thought it was—'

'Have you got a few minutes spare for us, Frau Bohlen?' asked Lena as Johann followed her into the room.

'Do I have a choice?'

Instead of replying, Lena sat down and waited for Johann to do the same. 'How was your relationship with Anna Bauer?'

'Good.'

'Was she committed to her job?'

'Of course. That's expected of all our employees. The home couldn't function otherwise.'

'You were perfectly happy with her performance?'

'I really don't see your point. Anna hasn't worked here in over six months. You know that.'

'Would you please answer my question?'

'I'd rather not.' Sabine Bohlen gave her a challenging look.

Lena took the voice recorder from her bag and placed it on the desk in front of Sabine Bohlen. 'Frau Bauer has come under suspicion of being connected with your husband's death. If you refuse to cooperate any further, I'll be forced to assume you were in on it.'

'DS Lorenzen, I—'

'DI Lorenzen, if you please.'

Sabine Bohlen seemed thrown. 'I beg your pardon?'

'My rank is detective inspector. If you must use it, please use the right one. One more time: were you perfectly happy with Anna Bauer's performance at work?'

'More or less,' Sabine Bohlen said at last. 'Her mind wasn't always on the job, but that's normal for young people.'

'We've heard that you'd known about your husband's affair for some time. Were you afraid your husband would divorce you?'

'Who said that?' hissed Sabine Bohlen.

'That's beside the point. Please answer the question.'

Sabine Bohlen glowered at Lena. 'No. No one was getting divorced. That's utter rubbish.'

'Was Frau Müller also sleeping with your husband?'

'Why don't you ask her?'

'We will, but right now I'm asking you.'

Sabine Bohlen said nothing for a moment. Finally, she looked into Lena's face, then almost immediately stared down at her hands and whispered, 'I don't know.'

Johann leaned forward and asked, 'Frau Bohlen, did you notice any signs that suggested she might be?'

She shot him a grateful look. 'Maybe. He was very friendly with her – too friendly, perhaps. I really don't know.'

'That's perfectly fine, Frau Bohlen. And how is your own relationship with Frau Müller? Did you or do you have any issues?'

'Sometimes she's a little . . . distant, but no – no real issues.'

Lena stood up and Johann followed suit.

'That'll be all for now.'

17

Lena leaned forward and made a point of placing the voice recorder on the table. She said the date and time and named the persons present.

'Why did you lie to us?' she asked without any further preamble. 'You met Anna Bauer and forced her to give up her job here.'

Isabel Müller inhaled sharply. 'Who says that?'

'I'm asking the questions. You answer. Is that clear?' said Lena harshly, glaring across at the young woman.

Isabel Müller raised her hands in defence. 'Look, what's all this about? Are you trying to pin something on me?'

'Did you know Anna Bauer before you applied for the position at the home?'

'I thought we could avoid all this. Yes, OK, we bumped into each other at a professional development seminar, but really only very briefly – a few of us sharing a drink at the hotel bar. We got talking. Just small talk. Shortly before she finished up here, she called me, told me she wanted out. I must have mentioned at the bar that I'd already applied to several children's homes, and maybe I even mentioned that I'd love to work in a place where folk go on holiday. Anyway, she called me and . . . you know the rest. She asked me not to tell anyone that we'd met. I kept my promise, that's all – it honestly didn't seem that much of a big deal. Sorry if I was wrong.'

'You paid Anna Bauer a considerable sum to give up her job.'

'I did what? Well, that's not true for a start. Why on earth would I do something like that? I didn't want the job that badly. It sounded great, that's true, but to have to pay for it . . . ?'

'We'll have the court order tomorrow at the latest to check your bank accounts. It'd be far better if you were open with us right now.'

'It's the God's honest truth. You're welcome to check my bank accounts, but you won't find much in there. You don't get rich from being a caregiver.'

'What exactly did Anna Bauer tell you? When did she contact you?'

'She called about a week before she handed in her resignation. They'd given out a list with our phone numbers at the seminar, you see.'

'When and where was the seminar?'

'About two years ago? Early August, I think – four days at the uni in Münster. I'd have to check the exact dates.'

'That info should be enough for us to go on,' Johann said.

'Great, then you'll soon find out that I'm telling the truth.'

'Just because you met at a seminar it doesn't mean you didn't pay Frau Bauer,' Lena said. 'Frau Bauer was very clear in her statement. I can only advise you to tell us everything right now.'

'You're repeating yourself,' Isabel Müller replied tartly.

'Do you have any medical knowledge?' asked Johann suddenly.

'What do you mean? You know what I do here.'

'Well, have you ever worked in a hospital?'

'I had an internship as a student, if you can call that work.'

'And how long was this internship?' asked Johann.

'One semester – about four months.'

'That's quite long for an internship. Was it linked to a particular course or apprenticeship?'

'Not really. Like I said, I was just an intern.'

'Is that the only professional contact you've had with the medical world?' asked Johann.

'I really don't know what you want from me.'

Lena noticed that Isabel Müller steered away from Johann's questions as much as she could, but she didn't see the need to pursue the point any further at this stage. 'I'd like to talk some more about your relationship with Hein Bohlen. We've heard statements suggesting that your relationship with him was more intimate than you've previously led us to believe.'

'And what exactly is your question?' Isabel Müller stared at them in defiance.

Lena continued unperturbed, 'Would you please describe your relationship with Hein Bohlen for us again?'

'If I must. I already told you yesterday that our relationship was purely professional. I had no problems with him and I don't think he had any with me. We were on first-name terms in spite of the age difference and we got on well. Is that enough for you?'

'He never wanted more?' asked Johann.

'I can imagine what you're thinking. Young, reasonably attractive woman flirts with her boss. A quickie on the desk or maybe in the kids' toilets. Is that what you want me to say?'

'If that's what happened,' Johann said without batting an eyelid. 'Are you seriously trying to tell us Herr Bohlen didn't show the slightest interest in you? From what we've learned about him, that seems highly unlikely.'

'Whatever! You can think what you like, but do you want me to make up a few hair-raising tales just to keep you happy? You can't be serious!'

'Why did your brother kill himself?' asked Lena. She'd fixed on the question because it was proving difficult to catch the imperturbable Isabel Müller off balance.

'That's none of your bloody business!' Isabel now snapped at Lena.

'I'm sorry, Frau Müller. We need to explore all avenues in the course of a murder investigation. Did his suicide have anything to do with his time living in children's homes?'

'Pure cod psychology. Is that what they teach you at police school? I'm not saying another word.'

'Why did you lie to us? You told us you were unemployed when you happened to come across this position.' Lena decided to change subject again because she realised Isabel Müller would remain silent about her brother until they could produce hard evidence.

'Unemployed? You must have misheard me.'

Johann cleared his throat and turned back a few pages in his little book. 'I quote from my notes: you were out of a job, heard about this position by chance, called the home and came for an interview the next day, then started one week later.'

Isabel Müller seemed rattled for an instant. 'No, surely I didn't say that. It wouldn't have been the truth.'

'Frau Müller,' Lena said tensely. 'You are facing two experienced criminal detectives. You can rest assured that your statement was recorded correctly. You lied during your very first interview with us. Now why would that be?'

'I really didn't. I've no idea what happened there. You don't get interviewed by the police every day – it's only normal to mix up details here and there. I've been out of work several times and had to find a new position. I must have got muddled in all the excitement.'

'You didn't appear at all excited,' Johann said. 'I even made a note of it.'

'That's ridiculous. Notes! You have no idea.' Isabel Müller was talking more to herself than to the two detectives.

'Did you know Herr Bohlen before you came here?' asked Lena. 'Why did you want to work here so badly that you gave up a steady job? That does not look like a coincidence in my book.'

Isabel Müller took her time. Lena thought the young woman seemed suddenly far away. 'There are so many coincidences in life,' she murmured.

'We can't see any reason why Anna Bauer wouldn't be telling the truth. How much did you pay her to quit her job?'

'I already told you. What do you want from me?' She touched her head. 'I feel sick. I need to lie down.'

Lena exchanged a glance with Johann and decided to carry on with the interview in the afternoon. Picking up the voice recorder, she said, 'Taking a break in the interview with Isabel Müller,' before switching the machine off. 'Have a lie-down. We'll come back around three p.m. this afternoon to continue this conversation. Do you understand, Frau Müller?'

Isabel Müller nodded, stood up and left the room without another word.

Lena and Johann's phones buzzed almost simultaneously. Lena had new emails from both DSU Warnke and Leon. When she looked up, Johann said, 'Forensics have the results on Bohlen's clothes, and we have the intel on the Hamburg licence plate. What about you?'

'Let's go back to the house. I hate reading emails on the phone.'

Fifteen minutes later, they were seated with their laptops at the kitchen table with the coffee machine hissing and spluttering in the background.

Lena opened Warnke's email, which had two lists attached, one itemising all the phones connected to the local network following the discovery of Hein Bohlen's corpse, and the other showing Reimers' phone record from that evening. Lena studied his list of calls, immediately spotting that he had not told the truth regarding the missing twenty minutes. At nine minutes past eleven he'd called Herbert Bergendorf's number and talked to him for seven minutes.

Lena gestured to Johann and he sat down beside her to look through the data for himself. 'Wow! You were bang on about that Bergendorf. I doubt Sergeant Reimers called to wish him goodnight. Did he seriously think we weren't going to find out?'

Lena opened the other list. More than sixty phones had been connected that evening. They skimmed through the list but could find no one relevant – neither Isabel Müller, Anna Bauer nor Sabine Bohlen.

'Your friend from school isn't there either,' Johann said. 'We'll have to talk to each one of these callers. That's going to take ages.'

Johann returned to his laptop and Lena read her second email. Leon had attached a letter from a doctor detailing the medical history of Isabel Müller's brother, Florian. Reading through the seven pages, Lena found several sections referring to Florian Müller's time at various homes. The doctor seemed to think the boy had been exposed to violence as a child, most likely combined with sexual assault. Florian Müller hadn't fully confided in the doctor and the medical professional made it very clear that he was merely speculating.

Lena decided to read the letter again in peace that evening – she might glean more from a second read. Right now she wanted to know what homes Florian Müller had stayed in and if there was any chance he'd crossed paths with Hein Bohlen. Lena delegated the task to Johann and focussed on Leon's other attachment. It was a chatroom transcript. Leon had texted her an explanation earlier – he preferred this split method of communicating when the intel was highly sensitive. His text message read:

Dark Web chat. Got password and username. Our man is Berg.
Be careful! You're stirring up a real hornets' nest.

Lena opened up the transcript. It appeared that five participants – one of them with the username Berg – had met at an agreed time on the Dark Web. She read:

Beil: Everyone well?

Rose: Let's get to the point. I don't have much time.

Schwarz: Berg, can you summarise, please.

Berg: Things are getting out of hand. You already know the CID is on the island. The bitch will get the phone records from our friend in Kiel tomorrow. I couldn't prevent it. That idiot called me on his work phone. The bitch won't give up.

Weiss: I always said that village copper is a risk.

Schwarz: No point in crying over spilled milk. Berg, how much does he know?

Berg: Enough to bring me down. The coward will try anything to save his own skin. We should never have contacted him directly.

Beil: Getting your knickers in a twist and moaning won't help. Schwarz asked precisely how much the copper's aware of.

Berg: Almost nothing. I don't think he has the brains to see through our business model, but he does know we had an interest in HB. I think we should get rid of him.

Beil: Get rid of him?

Schwarz: I agree. He needs to be got out of the picture ASAP. Berg, you're in charge of that.

Rose: OK, that's that sorted. But our investment hasn't paid off at all. No chance of going into business with the widow, is there?

Schwarz: No, no chance.

Beil: We'll have to write it off.

Schwarz: Frankly, that's the least of our concerns. I'm worried about the CID bitch. I've asked around about her. She won't give up once she's on to something.

Weiss: Can we contain the risk?

Schwarz: So far. We're well secured.

Weiss: We should have written off HB much sooner. I was always against asking for the money back.

Beil: It was a majority vote. Stop whingeing.

Rose: When's the next shipment due?

Schwarz: I cancelled everything. We need to lie low for now.

Berg: The CID bitch needs someone to pin the murder on.

Weiss: How are we going to manage that?

Schwarz: Not every case gets solved and she has limited time on the island. I'll see if I can speed things up.

Weiss: Good. I don't like what's been happening lately.

Berg: No one does, but we couldn't predict everything. The back payments were supposed to pile on the pressure. Who'd have thought the idiot would actually pay the first instalments? Everything would have turned out fine if he hadn't suddenly dropped dead.

Weiss: Would have, if – that's no good to us now.

Schwarz: Oh, stop bickering, all of you. We're well secured. This little glitch can't touch us.

Weiss: Let's hope to God you're right . . .

Rose: Is the shipment stored appropriately in the meantime?

Berg: All sorted.

Schwarz: I'll call a meeting in HH if necessary.

Berg: No problem. I'll need a day's notice.

Schwarz: Great. Any more questions? If not, we can finish up for today.

When Lena showed the transcript to Johann, he was speechless for a moment. 'Where did you get that?'

'The Dark Web. Berg is Herbert Bergendorf. I don't know the rest of their identities.'

'Then how did you identify Bergendorf? If you can do it with him, you—'

'Not possible, unfortunately.'

'No way! You – or whoever – hacked his computer without a court order? Are you insane? This guy has connections – even inside the police force, if I understand this chat correctly.'

'You're right, but tell me what judge would give us an order without proof? We have to do the groundwork ourselves. Don't worry, you've got nothing to do with this. If I get in trouble, I'll keep you out of it.'

'Great – well, that's me feeling perfectly reassured about it now.'

'Let's focus on the job in hand, OK? What else have you got?'

For a brief moment, Johann looked as though he was going to carry on arguing, but then he cleared his throat and said, 'You asked me to look into the alleged rape of a holidaymaker near the home. The case was scrapped because there was no case. The woman admitted later that she'd made it all up – that's the trouble with rumours. Next, the results came in from Forensics on Hein Bohlen's clothes: besides the funeral director, they found DNA from another male. I was told it must have been more than a mere handshake.'

'A fight, then? But there were no bruises on Bohlen's body.'

'Then it was something a little less than a fight. Either way, we have nothing to compare the sample with.'

'Which leads me on to the black hole in the timeline. Just who did Bohlen go to meet down there on the beach? Bearing in mind the chatroom conversation, I'd say it was Bergendorf. I wonder how Bohlen was connected with this shady group and why they gave him the eight hundred thousand euros as a kind of loan?'

'What did he have to offer on his side?'

'Children.'

'You mean . . . ?'

'Seems the most likely scenario to me. A children's home is hardly a lucrative investment –

as a money-laundering outfit maybe, but then the tax office would have noticed. All their income comes from public funds, doesn't it, and there'd be contracts and records.'

'Didn't the accountant say the home wasn't running at capacity in the beginning? How does that fit into the picture?'

'Did Bohlen need the space for children from other sources, I wonder?' Seeing Johann's expression, Lena added, 'I know it sounds horrible, but to people like that, children are goods.'

'Is that why you wanted me to find out if Isabel's brother was ever in a home where Hein Bohlen was working? But what could she have to do with this group?'

'I don't know. How soon can we find out?'

'I've passed it on to Flensburg, but it'll take a while. I don't even know if they can access this kind of information without a court order.'

'What else have you come up with?'

'The Hamburg licence plate belongs to a vehicle from a Hamburg import and export company. Do you want me to send someone over there?'

'No, best to let sleeping dogs lie for now, I think. Plus, we don't even know that Frau Müller wasn't chucking us a red herring to keep us busy and show her willingness to cooperate. First off, that Sergeant Reimers has some explaining to do and, after that, we'll pay Herr Bergendorf a visit.'

'So I'm not going to Föhr to check out Anna Bauer's alibi then?'

'Leave it to our colleagues on Föhr. If we still have any doubts, we'll just have to go over tomorrow.'

'OK, I'm on to it. I'll be ready in ten.'

18

A young constable opened the door at the police station. Lena held up her pass and asked for Walter Reimers.

'I'm sorry. He called in sick today.'

'In that case, we need his home address.'

After a brief hesitation, the constable told them the street and number. 'He's in the top flat. Do you want me to call and let him know you're on the way?'

'No thanks, we'll do that ourselves.'

Back in the car, Johann said, 'I bet you anything Sergeant Reimers won't be home.'

'And I bet you're right,' Lena said, starting the engine.

Quarter of an hour later, they were standing outside a three-storey apartment building. There was no answer to the buzzer, so Lena tried the other four on the panel. Eventually, a female voice replied, and Lena said, 'Lorenzen, police. Will you open the door, please?'

An elderly lady of around seventy met them in the stairwell. 'Police? Do you have any ID?'

'Right here, Frau Benzen.'

The elderly lady studied Lena's police pass. 'The name sounds familiar,' she said.

'That's because you were my German teacher in primary school.'

Frau Benzen beamed at Lena. 'Well I never! And here you are now with the police. I always thought you'd end up doing something with languages – you had such a knack, but look just how wrong I was. I expect this isn't a social call?'

'No, I'm afraid not. We need to speak with our colleague, Sergeant Reimers. He lives on the floor above you.'

'Yes, he does. But Herr Reimers isn't home at the moment. He dropped by with his key earlier on, because I always water his plants when he's away and empty his letterbox so it doesn't clog up.'

'Did he say how long he'll be away for?'

'He said he didn't know yet – work, apparently, and he might be gone a few weeks. He took a big suitcase when he left the house. I'm really sorry you came all the way for nothing.'

'Can't be helped, Frau Benzen.' Lena gave her a card. 'Would you please call me if Herr Reimers comes back in the next few days?'

'Of course, Lena. What a lovely surprise to see you again after all these years.'

Lena said goodbye to her old teacher and then she and Johann left the house.

'Shall we get him tracked down?' asked Johann.

'On what grounds? I'm guessing he'll call in sick and send in a medical certificate from some fancy clinic far away – burn-out or God knows what – and the doctor in charge won't allow us to talk to him.' Lena called the only number they had for Reimers, but it went straight to voicemail. She slammed her hand on the steering wheel in frustration. 'Dammit. They got him out of the way.'

'Nothing we can do in that case, I guess,' Johann said. 'We'll have to wait for the medical certificate.'

'Yep, the bird has flown.'

'Herbert Bergendorf next?'

'He's slippery as an eel. What are we going to accuse him of? Talking to a policeman?' Lena started the engine.

'Is there any actual point in following that lead? Sure, Reimers has got something going on with the guy, but does it have anything to do with Bohlen's death? Seems like two unrelated matters to me. We could get someone else to look into Bergendorf.'

Lena turned the engine back off. '"Seems like" – you may well have picked the right words there. We still don't know where Bohlen headed after he went to the supermarket or who he was meeting. If he was killed by a slow-acting poison, Bergendorf could be our man.'

'But then he lied to his chatroom buddies.'

'Well, he was running Bohlen for the group. What if Bohlen threatened to expose Bergendorf, and Bergendorf was afraid of his business partners? They don't strike me as the kind of people to muck around. So then he decided to take matters into his own hands.'

'Too many "might haves" for me,' Johann said. 'I think the other leads are a little more solid. Practically every woman at the children's home has a motive.'

'Don't worry, we'll keep on top of those too.' Lena started the engine again and drove off. 'Let's go and visit Herr Bergendorf.'

◆ ◆ ◆

'Someone's got plenty of dough,' Johann commented as they pulled up outside Bergendorf's house. They got out of the car, rang the bell and waited for over a minute before the owner opened the door.

'More questions, DI Lorenzen? And you even brought a colleague along this time.'

Lena introduced Johann. 'Do you have a moment?'

'Of course. My schedule isn't so busy these days, since my retirement. Please, come on in.' He stepped aside and waited for Lena and Johann to enter. 'We can sit in the library again. Can I offer you a coffee or tea this time?'

'No, thanks,' Lena said, walking ahead.

Herbert Bergendorf waited for the two detectives to take their seats before sitting down himself. 'How can I be of assistance?'

'We checked the phone records for the evening of the twenty-ninth of May and your number came up.'

'Quite likely. I enjoy talking on the phone.'

'Do you recall the conversation?'

'What time was this exactly?'

Lena looked at Johann, who was already leafing through his faithful notebook. At last he said, 'It was nine minutes past eleven. The connection lasted seven minutes.'

'That's more than two weeks ago now. I'm afraid I don't remember. As I said, I enjoy chats on the phone.'

Johann cleared his throat. 'Excuse me, Herr Bergendorf. May I just use your bathroom?'

'Of course. Second door on the right.'

Once Johann was out of the room, Herbert Bergendorf turned back to Lena. 'Do you have any further questions?'

'I'd rather wait for my colleague, if you don't mind.'

'No problem. Are you sure I can't get you something to drink?'

'I heard you're a great supporter of institutions and charities on behalf of children and young people – residential children's homes in particular,' Lena said without replying to his question.

'DI Lorenzen, I've been in retirement for over three years now. My bank offered financial support to a multitude of projects, no doubt including a good number in the youth sector.'

'Oh, I must have got the wrong end of the stick: I'd got the distinct impression that you'd been personally involved.' Johann returned to the library. 'OK, let's continue. On the twenty-ninth of May, Herr Bohlen had two . . . let's call them appointments, but we don't know who with.'

'I told you before that I last saw Herr Bohlen at least four weeks ago.'

'Yes, I know. But now we have a witness who claims to have seen you with Herr Bohlen on that very day.'

For the first time, Herbert Bergendorf seemed irritated. He swallowed and took a deep breath. 'A witness? And who's that supposed to be? Whoever it is, they're wrong.'

'So you didn't meet with Herr Bohlen that day?' asked Lena.

'No, as I already told you. Who's this witness supposed to be?'

'I'm sure you understand we can't discuss the details of our investigation, but we believe our witness is one hundred per cent reliable.'

'You can believe all you like, but that doesn't change the fact that your witness made a mistake.'

Studying Herbert Bergendorf's every move and twitch, Lena felt certain that he was properly rattled. His eyes jumped from her to Johann and then back again, and his fingers thrummed on the desk.

'Will that be all?' he asked, rising to his feet.

Lena and Johann followed suit. 'For the meantime, yes. Please make sure we can get hold of you over the next few days. We may have more questions. We're only at the very start of our investigation.'

There was no reply from Herbert Bergendorf. The two detectives nodded in farewell and left the house. Once inside the car, Johann held up a small ziplock bag. 'This might tell us more,' he said, jiggling the hair in the bag. 'Although we can't use this officially either.'

'Would you look at that? The boy is learning,' Lena said with a smirk.

'Did your mole in Flensburg not tell you my nickname?'

'My *mole*? That's a bit strong. But yes, my associate in Flensburg did tell me a thing or two about you. But don't worry, they've called me worse.'

Johann grinned. 'I can imagine.'

'Watch it – very thin ice.'

Johann was about to reply when his phone buzzed. He checked the display. 'Could be an email about the homes Florian Müller was put in as a child.' He opened the email and nodded. 'Bullseye, but I need to double-check this against the list on my laptop.'

'What now?' asked Johann after he'd compared the lists back at the house. Shortly after Florian Müller was separated from his sister, he'd been placed in a home near Osnabrück – where Hein Bohlen was serving as deputy manager.

'Does the home still exist?' asked Lena.

Johann searched online and soon found that the home had closed ten years ago. An article from the archive of a local newspaper in Osnabrück suggested there'd been irregularities.

'*Irregularities*,' Johann muttered. 'Is that what you call it?'

'We need to find out more. I suggest you go to Osnabrück and do a bit of digging. I'll notify DSU Warnke right now so he can tell our colleagues in Lower Saxony that you're on your way.'

'OK!' Johann picked up the ferry timetable. 'If you take me over to Wittdün now, I'll be in Osnabrück by tonight and back here by tomorrow afternoon. I'll drop the hair sample in at the station in Husum on the way and ask them to send it off to Flensburg right away. With a bit of luck, we'll have a result the day after tomorrow.'

Lena grabbed the car keys. 'Sounds good.'

Lena returned to Norddorf early in the afternoon, dropped the car at the house and walked to the Strandhalle restaurant. She grabbed a bite to eat and hired a beach chair close to the water, then settled in with her laptop and the case files.

She'd called Warnke on her drive back from Wittdün and asked him to inform the Osnabrück police station about Johann's forthcoming visit.

The tide was rising, the sun had been out since noon and temperatures were just above twenty degrees. Lena sank back in the beach chair and closed her eyes, replaying her conversation with Warnke in her head.

'You'd stand a better chance if you could actually find a witness who saw Bergendorf with Bohlen at the time in question,' he'd replied to Lena's query about getting a search warrant for Bergendorf's house. She hadn't told him about the Dark Web chat or about her suspicion regarding child abuse. 'You're going to have to find another way,' he'd said. 'Bearing in mind these people hire the best lawyers, they'll make sure we won't be able to use any evidence you've come by off the record.'

Warnke had never spoken so openly with her before and Lena understood more and more why he'd sent her to Amrum rather than anyone else. For some reason, her unconventional methods seemed to suit him just fine in this case, not to mention the fact that she was willing to take greater risks than her colleagues.

When she'd asked him how far she could rely on him if push came to shove, he'd paused for a long moment before replying, 'I'll do everything in my power, but it might not be enough.'

Had Hein Bohlen really been poisoned? Had the Institute for Tropical Medicine in Hamburg genuinely been charged with identifying a mysterious poison? Or was it all staged, an act designed to gain time? Did Bohlen die a natural death after all? Were they committing a huge injustice in suspecting the women at the home? Could it be coincidence that Florian Müller had lived at the same home Hein Bohlen had worked at? The circumstances surrounding Anna Bauer's sudden resignation suggested it wasn't. Perhaps they needed to rethink the whole case: that there was no poisoning. If it was indeed murder, it had been done in some other way that didn't presuppose experience with handling poisons. Lena reached for her phone and called Luise Stahnke in Forensics.

'Lena, hi. Still on the island?'

'Hi, Luise. Yes, and it looks like I'll be here for a while yet.'

'What do you want to know?'

Lena smiled. The pathologist in Kiel knew her better than to think she'd called for a chat. 'I've gone off the poison theory.'

'Hear, hear.'

'But if it's still murder, I need a different method. Is there any conceivable way someone might have given him something that caused the heart attack a few hours later? The man was known to have a heart condition, after all.' Lena listed the medications Hein Bohlen had been taking.

'Yes, they're all typically prescribed in such a case. To answer your question, it's possible in theory, but something like that is hard to come by and usually fast-acting. The dosage would have to be measured precisely for that person. Any doctors or pharmacists among your suspects?'

'Not at this stage.'

'Then I'd put this theory way at the bottom of your list.'

'What would your advice be to a potential killer going down this route?'

'To find a way to drop the beta blockers. Gradually, not all at once, as that would bring on immediate complications and the murderer would be in danger of being discovered right away. Blood pressure would slowly rise, and if the shit hit the fan – say if the victim got massively upset or stressed out, for example – you'd get your heart attack and it'd look completely natural. Still, it'd be the most unlikely way to finish someone off I've ever come across. But let's assume for a moment someone actually put this crazy idea into practice, was your victim under a lot of pressure? Did he blow his top easily?'

'Yes, basically he'd be just the right type for such a murder. I'd wondered before if someone might have swapped his pills, but I can't see how anyone could produce fake blister packs with the original name and label of the medication.'

'I agree – seems practically impossible unless they have contacts with someone in the criminal underworld who happens to produce fake meds, including precisely the one the murderer needs. I'm sorry I can't be of more help, but you did ask . . .'

'I know, Luise. I needed your honest opinion.'

'So to recap, your victim was under a lot of stress?'

'Good question. He definitely changed in the weeks leading up to his death. Almost everyone we interviewed said so. He took out a shedload of cash from his account and we don't know who or what for, but if my suspicions are correct, he stood to lose everything he'd been working for. The trouble is, I just can't prove it.'

'In that case, he may not have needed his medication to be tampered with to have a heart attack, which means no murder and no killer.'

'That thought had crossed my mind, though there is evidence pointing to the contrary. Either way, you've helped me lots.'

'Any time! Call me when you're back in Kiel. We haven't had a proper girls' night out in ages.'

Lena laughed. 'Great, but only if we've got the next day off, or I might lose my job over alcohol abuse and you'll miss some decisive clue in the hunt for your next villain.'

'OK, why don't we make it a Friday then. Call me?'

Lena promised to be in touch as soon as she was back in the city and hung up.

19

Lena read carefully through every file and all of Johann's detailed reports. She couldn't shake off the sense that she was missing something – that some vital clue lay right there in front of her eyes and she simply wasn't seeing it. Some crucial point that would move the whole investigation forward.

She couldn't find anything in the files. It must be something she'd come across on the margins of their investigation, or possibly entirely beyond the scope of the investigation itself. She closed the folder and her laptop.

Johann had texted half an hour ago to say he was nearly in Osnabrück and had arranged to meet with a retired detective that evening.

Lena called her aunt.

'Hello, *deern*,' the elderly lady said. 'How are you?'

'Hi, Beke. I'm not sure if I can make it today.'

'Don't worry about it. I imagine your job is keeping you on your toes.'

'My colleague's away until tomorrow. How about I take you out for breakfast in the morning?'

'That sounds wonderful.'

'Is eight too early?'

'Child, I get up at six every day. Why should eight be too early?'

'I'm sorry, Beke, I wasn't thinking.' Lena's phone buzzed to show there was a call waiting. 'I have to go now, Beke. Someone's trying to call me. I'll pick you up in the morning.' She hung up and took the other call.

'Where are you?'

'Oh, hi, Erck. Take a guess!' She held the phone up so he could hear the wind and the waves.

'Sounds like you've invested in one of those gorgeous beach chairs. Got room for one more?'

'If I just shift my laptop and papers . . .'

'I'll be there in ten,' he said and hung up.

'Well, that's the end of my quiet evening,' Lena muttered, curling into a corner. She'd brought a blanket from the house and now wrapped herself up in it. She'd been pushing thoughts of Erck aside all day, but now she was lost in the memories of last night. She'd enjoyed lying in his strong arms once more, listening to his deep voice and the beating of his heart. Had she really thought Erck would drop it after this single night together? She knew how persistent he could be when he wanted something. Maybe last night had been a fresh start rather than the long-overdue farewell?

'What are you thinking about?'

Lena opened her eyes to find Erck in front of her, a broad smile on his face and two steaming paper cups in his hands. 'Beach chair service. Café latte, my lady?' He sat down beside her and handed her a cup. 'Freshly made.'

'My hero! Thank you so much.'

'That's what you used to call me years ago. Remember?'

'Did you think I'd forgotten about our time together?'

He took a sip from his coffee. 'No idea what I thought, really. I tried to block it out, in a way. It was the only way for me to cope with it.'

'With it?'

He sighed. 'With the loss,' he said at last. Then he added softly, 'That's how it was for me – as if you'd died. At least then I could have mourned you.'

'And what do we do now?'

'You tell me.'

'Closure evening number two?'

Erck said nothing, drained the last drops from his cup and placed it down in the sand. 'Can I come under your blanket?'

Erck gently ran his hand over Lena's stomach. After an hour in the beach chair they'd gone back to Lena's accommodation, and after a brief interlude in the kitchen had ended up in bed.

'You're so beautiful,' he said. 'Even more beautiful than back then.'

'Don't talk nonsense. Have you forgotten how old we are now?'

'You make it sound like we're about to go into retirement. We're in the prime of our lives.'

'No more silly ideas in our heads, you mean?'

'Did we have those before?'

Lena shrugged and snuggled up closer to Erck. 'I can't remember. Repressed memory or something like that.'

'Sure, that makes two of us. We should team up – we'd be unstoppable!'

'At repressing things?'

'Yes; our past would be completely erased and we could start afresh.'

'Nutcase,' Lena mumbled.

'I'm serious. I mean, what's stopping us from starting over?'

Lena sat up. 'I thought this subject was off limits?'

Erck pulled Lena back down and kissed her on the mouth. 'Are you afraid I'll move to Kiel with you?'

'No, you'd never leave the island. Why should I be afraid of that?'

'Do you have a boyfriend there?'

Lena hesitated. At last she said, 'Yes, kind of.'

'What does "kind of" mean? Is it a dog or a cat?'

'Joe. His name is Joe. He wants us to move in together and have children. He's a colleague from the Kiel constabulary.'

'You forgot about getting married.'

'True. That's supposed to happen between the two other things.'

'And what do you want?'

'None of the above.'

'Then you should tell him.'

'I know I should. But you know me, I'm not good at those things. Plus, our relationship would almost certainly be over if I did, and maybe I don't want that.'

'What's the big but? I don't know this Joe, but it sounds awfully like you're playing with him, and that's not fair. The Lena I know is always fair.'

Lena said nothing. She knew Erck had hit the nail right on the head. Then again, her relationship with Joe was none of his business. It had been a mistake to answer his question.

'Also off limits?' asked Erck, almost as though he'd read her thoughts.

'Am I that easy to read?'

'Perhaps I just know you too well.'

Wasn't that precisely why she felt so comfortable around him? Was that what she missed with Joe? Or were her feelings for Erck purely nostalgic, based on nothing but happy memories?

When Lena didn't reply, Erck said, 'I always wondered why every woman I met after you felt so distant. I'm not saying I was thinking of you all the time when I was with them, and I didn't compare them with you either. There's no point in that, because everyone's different. Still, there was always that something missing. Maybe it has to do with the fact that you and I both grew up here. You know what Amrum means to me, to us, and if things had been different, you wouldn't have run off the way you did, or at least you'd have come back sooner or later. D'you understand what I'm trying to say?'

Lena kissed him passionately. 'You do realise that was a declaration of love, don't you?' When Erck didn't reply, she added, 'But that was one of the loveliest I've ever heard.'

'That's a start,' he whispered and held her more closely to him.

Lena opened her eyes and looked into Erck's smiling face. 'Have you been awake long?'

'Yes.'

'Did you sleep at all?'

'Yes.'

'Can you say anything other than "yes"?'

'No,' he said and kissed her. 'Have you got time?'

Lena looked at the clock. It was just after six. 'An hour at least.'

'Perfect,' he said, covering her body in kisses.

Beke paused and looked in wonder at Lena as she opened the door. A huge smile on her face, her niece ran her fingers through her hair and asked, 'Is something wrong?'

Beke closed the door behind her and hugged her. 'No, not at all. You just look so happy. Have you caught the murderer?'

Lena turned quickly towards the car and muttered, 'No, not quite.'

Beke followed behind her. 'Are we in a hurry?'

Lena slowed down now she had her emotions halfway in check again. She hadn't wanted to show Beke how much her comment had taken her by surprise. Her aunt would have guessed in no time that her beaming smile was because of a man, not her job. And who else could that man be other than Erck? That aside, Beke had to be wrong. She felt exactly the same as any other day. Well, nearly.

'I'm sorry, I was daydreaming,' she said, taking her aunt's arm.

A short while later they were chatting over cappuccinos in a small café set in a traditional Frisian house. Beke told Lena about her two best friends, who had both lost their husbands within months of each other the previous year. Beke was helping the women get back on their feet and together they were volunteering for the local church and had created a small children's library. They went to concerts at the local hall and enjoyed a small tipple in one of Norddorf's many restaurants afterwards.

'Sound like you're three busy ladies,' Lena said.

'Yes, you could say that.' Beke turned serious. 'Your father came by yesterday. Someone told him you're on the island.'

Lena groaned.

'He asked me to put in a good word with you and—'

'Well, now you have, Beke,' Lena said, cutting her off.

'He'd really like to see you.'

'Sounds lovely. Then I can finally meet that fantastic woman – she must be, or else he'd hardly have cheated on Mum and driven her to her death.'

Lena had spoken quietly but her eyes blazed with fury.

Beke placed her hand on top of Lena's. 'I just didn't want to keep it from you, my love. Of course, you must decide these things for yourself.'

'I'm sorry, Beke, I didn't mean to snap at you, but for me this business is done and dusted.'

Her aunt said nothing.

'Let's talk about something else. But next time my dear biological relative pays you a visit, tell him what I just said – that's my final word on the subject.'

For a moment it seemed the mood between them had turned, but then Beke pulled Lena into her arms. '*Deern*, I do understand, you know. Your mother was my beloved sister.'

Lena kissed Beke's cheek. 'I know, my darling. I know.'

'And I don't mean to get involved, but when he was standing right there in front of me . . . Never mind. You're my last living relative and there's no way I'm going to lose you.'

'You won't. We're sticking together, you and me.'

Her eyes swimming with tears, Beke fished for a tissue in her handbag. She seemed suddenly to remember something and pulled out a pill organiser. 'Oh, I'd almost forgotten.'

Lena stared at the container. It was a box with separate compartments for each day, each one filled with loose pills.

'What's the matter, child? You know I need to take these for my digestion. The doctor says they're completely harmless.'

Lena nodded, deep in thought. She'd seen her aunt's pill organiser on her first visit and it hadn't registered, but now she was hit with the realisation that this was precisely the piece of the puzzle she'd been looking for. She leapt to her feet.

'Beke, I forgot something really important. I have to run.' She pulled a note from her wallet and placed it on the table in front of her astonished aunt. 'Will you pay for me, please? And do stay and enjoy the breakfast!'

'What happened, *deern*?'

'I'll tell you tomorrow.' She gave Beke a quick kiss goodbye and rushed out of the café.

Johann called while she was en route to the children's home, launching straight into his report. 'I've spoken with three colleagues, two of them retired. I'll email you the full report this afternoon, but I thought you'd want to hear the headlines straight away. There was an investigation into the home – allegations of sexual abuse against children and teenagers. The retired detective I spoke with last night was extremely forthcoming. An anonymous complaint was made during the time Florian Müller was at the home, and a cautious investigation was launched. The home had powerful benefactors and the investigating officers had to proceed very carefully, but they quickly hit a brick wall. The detective I met carried on, on his own initiative, and met up with a boy from the home. This boy hadn't himself been affected, but what he told the detective fitted the bill. Before he'd gathered enough evidence, however, all three children in question were moved on to different homes. The man was certain that Florian Müller was one of them. He handed over all his findings to his boss, but the whole affair was quietly hushed up and he was told to shut up or face a disciplinary. He gave up at that point, but – and you won't believe this – he passed on copies of all his findings to me. Our victim quite definitely played an active part in the proceedings back then.'

'Great work, Johann – truly, well done!'

'Thanks. But that's not all. I went to the constabulary this morning and checked the records. Guess who the chief prosecutor in charge of the case was?'

'Lübbers!'

'Damn right. Bit of a strange coincidence, isn't it? I spoke with two other detectives from that time, but they didn't have a lot to add. You know what it's like – no one likes to go out on a limb, especially not when all you have is rumours. I reckon we've got enough to ask Isabel Müller a few more questions, though.'

Lena agreed and told him about her suspicion regarding the pill organiser.

'Why didn't we think of that ages ago?'

'It's just a hunch so far but I'm on my way to the home to check it out. When are you back?'

'All being well, I should arrive back in Wittdün at two.'

'Bring your car. I'll text you where to find me.'

I have to make a decision now.
  I promised him.
  They won't get away with it.
  They can't get away with it.
  It's high time someone did something.
  I promised him.

20

Lena ran into Sabine Bohlen in the corridor. 'Oh, for goodness' sake, haven't you finished with us all yet?' the woman grumbled as she led the way to her office.

'And a good morning to you,' Lena replied. 'When we first visited, you showed us your husband's medication. Did he use a pill organiser?'

'Yes, why?'

'It's important to our investigation. How long had he been using one?'

'Well, he forgot to take his pills a couple of times and started having problems so I bought him the organiser.'

'Did he refill it himself?'

'No, I did.'

'I assume you removed the individual pills from the blister pack?'

'Of course, or they wouldn't have fitted.'

'Can I please see the organiser?'

Sabine Bohlen nodded and stood up. She was about to open a drawer on the sideboard when Lena stopped her and, snapping on a pair of latex gloves, opened it herself. The container lay on top of a bundle of papers and was still half full of pills. Lena slid the box into a ziplock bag and sealed it.

'What's this all about?' asked Sabine Bohlen.

'I'm confiscating the pill organiser as evidence – my suspicion is that someone swapped your husband's medication over a prolonged period of time.'

'But who on earth would have done such a thing?' Sabine's voice cracked.

'That's what I'm here to find out. Did you touch this box again following your husband's death?'

'No – why would I? Are you accusing me of giving Hein the wrong medicine?'

Lena gestured towards the table and chairs. 'Let's sit down for a moment, Frau Bohlen.'

Sabine Bohlen took a seat without looking at Lena.

Lena sat down with her. 'Who has access to your office?'

'I only lock it at night. In theory, anyone could come in during the day, although no one has any business being in here apart from my husband and me, and I've never seen any of our employees in here, nor the children.' She looked up. 'Are you trying to say it was me? That's outrageous.'

'I'm not trying to say anything. Is Frau Müller in?'

'No.'

'But?'

'She's on leave at the moment.'

'Please, Frau Bohlen – what exactly do you mean by that?'

'She came to see me yesterday and asked for a few days off. Her uncle died and she has to make all the arrangements. It's extremely inconvenient, but what was I supposed to do?'

'So she's left Amrum?'

'Unless the uncle happened to live around here, I guess so,' snapped Sabine Bohlen.

Lena rose to her feet. 'Can you please give me Frau Müller's phone number?'

'I'm not sure she—'

'Now would be good.'

Stony-faced, Sabine Bohlen walked over to her desk and jotted the details down on a piece of paper. 'There you go.'

Lena called the number and left a message on voicemail before hanging up. 'I'm going to order a search warrant for the home and for Frau Müller's room: I expect it to come through within half an hour. I need you to leave the office now and ask you not to return to your flat. Do you understand?'

Sabine Bohlen gaped in shock at Lena and eventually hissed, 'I promise you now, there will be consequences.'

DSU Warnke caught on quickly and promised Lena that he would request the warrant right away and get back to her in ten minutes. Sabine Bohlen had left the office cursing and was waiting in the common room. As soon as Warnke gave Lena the OK, she called Nebel police station and requested the assistance of the two constables. They turned up fifteen minutes later and Lena told them what to look for. She took on Isabel Müller's room herself.

It was a small, plain room, simply furnished. A narrow bed stood along the right-hand wall below the only window, with a wardrobe alongside it. On the opposite wall stood a desk and chair, beneath a shelf with a few books and a small box. A laptop sat on the desk. Lena started it up and breathed a sigh of relief when it didn't ask for a password. She pulled out her phone.

Leon didn't pick up for a long while. 'Are you crazy? It's early!'

'I'm sitting in front of a laptop. I'm in, but I need to find something quickly. Can you help me, please?'

Lena followed Leon's instructions to install TeamViewer software and granted him access. 'I'm looking for any clues that she tried to find out about medication to lower blood pressure. And anything else weird that might come up.'

'Sure . . . weird. Do you have any idea how weird *most* people are?'

'Talk to you shortly, Leon,' Lena said, ignoring his question, and hung up.

She did a systematic search, starting with the wardrobe. It contained the type of clothing you'd expect to find in a young woman's room. Lena emptied one shelf after the other but found nothing suspicious. Finally, she pulled the wardrobe away from the wall to check behind it. She was about to push it back into place when she noticed a small plastic bag taped against the bottom of the wardrobe. Lena unpeeled it carefully and held it up to the light. The bag contained a handful of white pills, very similar to those in the organiser.

Before continuing with her search, she rang DSU Warnke and asked him to pinpoint the location of Isabel Müller's phone. Next she searched the desk, but found nothing of interest. On the bookshelf she came across several letters written by Florian Müller. Skimming through them confirmed Lena's suspicion that he was in psychiatric treatment because of something that had happened during his time in children's homes as a boy. He never said so explicitly, but it was clear that it must have been something dreadful.

Lena called Leon again. 'Found anything?'

'Oh yes, there's always something to find.'

'And?'

'She did extensive research on beta blockers via patient forums, among other places. She wanted to know how they worked and what experiences users had with them. She also visited the Dark Web, but didn't get very far. And she's a member of a secret online group for victims of those dirty bastards.'

'Victims of paedophiles, you mean?'

'What else? She asked a lot of questions and people asked her things in return. The name Lübbers mean anything to you? Chief prosecutor in Kiel.'

'Can you write me a quick report on that?'

'Link's on its way,' he said, hanging up.

Lena continued her search, sealed off the room and then went to help her colleagues investigate Sabine Bohlen's private quarters. After another hour she concluded the search, sealed off the office and told Sabine Bohlen she could return to her flat. The crime scene investigators from Flensburg would come tomorrow at the latest to examine the sealed rooms more thoroughly. If Isabel Müller ended up in court and did not confess, the prosecution would need to be based on circumstantial evidence.

Lena was startled when she checked the time. It was nearly two. She sent a quick text to Johann, asking him to come straight to their house when he arrived back on Amrum. Next, she gave the two constables a photo of Isabel Müller and sent them off to the ferry terminal, one to question the staff and the other to check every passenger leaving the island. Lena had also put in a request for two more constables from Föhr, who'd be arriving that afternoon.

'So we're zeroing in on Isabel Müller?' asked Johann when he joined Lena at the kitchen table.

'I doubt she'll be charged with more than manslaughter, though. I suspect she lowered the dose very gradually and it wouldn't have come to a heart attack without external influence. If he'd been with his wife at the time, he might have been saved.'

'The intent to kill was definitely there, though. Now we just need to get hold of her. No luck in locating her phone yet?'

'No, but I'm in constant touch with the expert at the CID. The moment she switches on her phone we'll know where she is – or at least where her phone is. The CSI will be on the first ferry in the morning to check the rooms over again. We can't do anything more for the moment.'

'Do you think she's still on Amrum?'

'I don't know. Why didn't she leave the island before? She could have quit, called in sick, whatever. Why hang around and wait for Bohlen's death to be investigated? She'd achieved her goal.'

'Hmm, you're right. It does seem odd.'

'Unless she's not done. She wanted to punish Hein Bohlen for what happened to her brother. I think we can assume with reasonable certainty that Florian was sexually abused as a boy. Bearing that in mind, along with the chatroom transcript, I reckon we're dealing with a child-trafficking ring.'

'Which means Herbert Bergendorf is in danger – if Isabel Müller found out about him, that is.'

Lena stood up. 'You're right. Let's go.' She grabbed her gun from the table.

Outside, Johann headed towards his car.

'Let's go together,' said Lena, crossing to her Passat.

'I'll be right there. I'm just getting something.'

Climbing in next to Lena, he placed two bulletproof vests on the back seat. 'You never know.'

Meanwhile, Lena had put on the blue lights, switching the siren on once they reached the main road to warn other traffic and turning it off a little before Bergendorf's house. All seemed quiet from the outside. They bent low as they ran towards the building. Lena listened at the door and shook her head after a few seconds.

'Doorbell?' whispered Johann.

'It'd warn her if she's inside.'

Lena's phone vibrated. A call. She picked up and listened, then hung up. 'They located her phone. She's right here.'

Johann said nothing but handed Lena the second vest. He'd already put his on.

Lena gestured to the right. 'We'll go around the back. We might see her through a window.'

Johann nodded and followed her. The first window appeared to belong to the guest bathroom. Lena ducked forward to check, then leaned back again. 'Nothing,' she whispered and started to inch her way along, sticking close to the wall. Slowly, they made their way to the rear of the property, without finding any sign of life. Unlike the front of the house, which had been kept in Frisian style with small lattice windows, the living area had been modernised with huge floor-to-ceiling windows. The curtains were drawn and the detectives were unable to see inside.

'How long for a special unit to get here?' asked Johann.

'Depends if there's a helicopter available. An hour at least, probably more.'

'What do we do?'

Frantically, Lena ran over options for getting into the house. 'The guest bathroom. I have a glass cutter in the car.' Seeing the look on Johann's face, she added, 'I confiscated it a couple of weeks ago during a house search.'

'Oh, OK. Worth a try.'

Back at the front of the house, Lena scurried to her car, fetched the glass cutter from the boot and returned to the bathroom window. Carefully, she cut a hole in both panes of the double-glazing and gingerly reached inside to release the window catches. Climbing in with Johann's assistance, she realised she wouldn't have managed without him. Lena tiptoed to the door of the bathroom and peered out into the hallway. Everything seemed quiet. After listening a few seconds longer, she crept to the front door and tried the handle to let Johann in, but the door was locked with no key in sight. Lena texted Johann and asked him to call in the two island constables for support. She started moving quietly down the hallway, pausing to listen at each doorway. Finally, she heard something by the library and pressed her ear to the door, holding her breath. An aggressive female voice was barking out brief commands inside the room. Lena texted Johann again to say that she'd be sending him a message every three minutes from now on and set the timer on her phone as a reminder. Finally, with her gun in her right hand, she pressed down gently on the handle of the library door with her left. Feeling no resistance, she shoved the door open with her shoulder, yelling, 'Police!'

Sizing up the situation in an instant, she saw Herbert Bergendorf seated, his hands and feet taped to the chair, eyes wide with fear, beads of sweat on his brow. Next to him stood Isabel Müller with a long kitchen knife in her hand. The moment Lena entered the library, she held the knife against Bergendorf's throat.

'Stay calm,' Lena said, her eyes fixed on the hand with the knife so she could fire a shot at Isabel Müller if necessary.

'Get out!' the young woman shouted hysterically.

'We can talk about this, Frau Müller.'

'Like hell we can! Point your gun at this filthy pig instead so he opens his mouth.'

'What do you want from him?'

'To tell the truth. The whole truth about him and his dirty friends who rape little boys.'

'Has he confessed?'

Lena noticed the horror in Herbert Bergendorf's eyes when the meaning of her words sank in.

'Yes. Disgusting details from years of abusing innocent children.'

'Children like your brother, Florian.'

Isabel Müller swallowed and Lena saw her grip on the knife slacken, but the woman's focus returned a moment later. 'And so many more,' Isabel said, punching Bergendorf in the head with her left hand. 'Hear that, you filthy pig? How many little souls did you destroy?' She hit him again, screaming, 'How many?'

'I don't know,' Bergendorf whimpered. His breathing was shallow, his face contorted in fear.

'How many?'

'A hundred or more. A little more.'

'Frau Müller, I've heard the confession of this monster now. I stand as your witness. Now let him go so we can arrest him, along with the rest of his so-called friends.'

'You'd like that, wouldn't you, slut? I know exactly how it goes. I'll go down while the real crooks get away with it. I want names. I want to know everything now. Where it happened, when, how?' She punched Bergendorf again and he cried out.

Lena heard a noise behind her. Johann must have made it through the window. She only hoped he was a good shot and her plan wouldn't end in disaster. 'Frau Müller, I'm putting down my gun. See?' She crouched down slowly, placed her gun on the ground and rose gently back up to her feet before raising her hands in the air. 'I'm unarmed.'

'Push it away from you,' Isabel Müller hissed.

Lena slid her gun aside with her foot as far as she could. 'OK, now we can talk. You've done nothing wrong so far. On the contrary. You've done us a great favour and dragged a confession out of this bastard – we'd never have done it with our limited means. Once I've got him behind bars, it's only a matter of time before he tells me every single name and detail. Trust me, I've got years of experience and I've solved all my cases so far and caught every crook.'

'I don't believe any of it. You're lying.'

'No, Frau Müller. Why do you think I'm here then? How did I know to find you here? He's been on my radar for quite a while. I soon realised what your boss had going on. You know, I'm the CID's expert in cases involving sexual abuse of children. I've put a whole heap of monsters like him behind bars and I'm truly grateful you helped me get to the bottom of this case.'

'If what you're saying is true, then why didn't you say something before? You never said a word all this time!'

'We can't, Frau Müller. I'd lose my job if I did that. You do understand that, don't you?'

'Yes,' the other woman said awkwardly. 'Yes, of course.'

'You can rest assured we're watching this gang. Each and every member is going behind bars for many years – life, probably.'

As the detective continued to speak soothingly with his assailant, Herbert Bergendorf gradually seemed to realise what they were saying. Lena could tell it was dawning on him that he and his associates might in fact now be brought to justice.

'What the hell are you talking about?' he burst out. 'I'm the victim here. Do something, for Christ's sake!'

Isabel Müller flinched and Lena feared she'd use the knife.

'You miserable piece of shit!' she screamed at him. 'You, a victim? You've murdered hundreds of little souls! You don't deserve to live.' She raised the knife.

'Don't do it,' pleaded Lena, 'or we'll never find out who the others are.'

'I don't care,' hissed Isabel Müller.

Seeing that Isabel was about to bring down the knife, Lena yelled, 'Now, Johann!' and dropped to the floor. Johann appeared in the doorway, found his bearings in an instant and pointed his gun at Isabel Müller. Practically in the same second, Lena heard the shot ring out.

21

Lena and Johann watched as the air ambulance took off towards Husum.

'How far to the hospital?' asked Johann.

'By air? Around fifteen minutes at the most.'

'Do you think they'll make it?'

'Not sure about him. I don't think you need to worry about her, though. She didn't seem too badly wounded.'

'I didn't have much time to think it through,' he said, stricken with guilt.

'Listen, you did everything right. That idiot should have kept his mouth shut, then he'd have been fine.'

'How on earth did she still manage to stab him? I don't get it.'

Lena had been trying to reassure Johann ever since the emergency doctor had taken Isabel Müller under his care. After the initial shock, doubts had started to creep in, making him wonder if he could have acted differently: waited another second, shot her higher up the shoulder or in the arm, perhaps.

'You couldn't have done any better. Your shot was brilliant. Honestly, I don't know if I could have acted as fast as you did.'

'Do they have our number?' asked Johann for the second time.

Herbert Bergendorf had been taken to Husum on the first flight out. Lena had requested two constables from the local police there to keep a guard on his and Isabel's rooms at the hospital. Isabel's knife had left Bergendorf critically injured and Lena had struggled to stem the bleeding. Dr Neumann, who arrived a few minutes later, had bound the wound before handing Bergendorf over to the emergency doctor. Meanwhile, Isabel Müller was stabilised sufficiently to be taken off the island on a second flight.

'Yes, they do,' Lena said. 'You OK to catch a ride back to the house with one of the constables? I need to speak with Warnke.'

Johann nodded. 'Yes, sure.'

Lena pulled out her phone and watched as her young colleague walked over to one of the police cars.

'Lena, hello,' said Enno Eilts. 'Any news?'

Lena told her former boss about the events of the last few hours.

When she had finished, he said, 'Not the nicest thing to do, letting you walk straight into it.'

'I think that must have been Warnke's plan all along. Sending me here to make a lot of noise to frighten the gang into action. I assume there never was any poison and the Institute for Tropical Medicine in Hamburg was never likely to find any.'

'Yes, I agree. When they found nothing suspicious during the post-mortem, Warnke thought up another way to utilise the situation. He must have had his eye on Bohlen for a while.'

'Well, his plan worked out, I guess – partially, at least. I can only prove that the medication was swapped, though, and we don't even know yet what Isabel Müller's pills are. Hardly enough for a murder charge. I'm guessing Bergendorf put pressure on Bohlen and they met up on the day of his death – that has to be what finally triggered the heart attack. I'm hoping the DNA on Bohlen's clothes will confirm that.'

'Will Bergendorf live?'

'The doctor couldn't or wouldn't say, but judging by what he said to the local GP here, it's not looking good.'

'Case closed?'

Lena said nothing.

'That's a no then,' Enno Eilts said. 'Any idea how you might catch this gang of perverts?'

'My expert tells me it's impossible to track someone's activities on the Dark Web, but I do know how to get into the chatroom. I could call a meeting.'

'You want to set a trap?'

'Yes, but I can only do so if I'm granted official access to Bergendorf's laptop.'

'Hmm, tricky. He is the victim here.'

'And if I do it anyway?'

'You'd be taking a huge risk,' Enno Eilts replied. 'Is it really worth it?'

'It's high time someone put a stop to these people. They've been at it for at least ten years now, from the sound of it.'

'Warnke won't back you up if the going gets rough.'

'I know, but I don't see any other way.'

'Be careful, won't you?' Enno Eilts said at last, asking her to keep in touch.

Next on Lena's list of calls was Leon. 'I've got his laptop. Can you call in a meeting? I'd be "Berg".'

'And where is this guy?'

'On his way to hospital. He's got other things to worry about right now.'

'Great! When do you want it to happen?'

'I've got a few things to sort out first. I'll get back to you the moment I can.'

Leon hung up and Lena called Warnke.

'So what's the situation?'

Lena filled him in on what had happened. 'Bergendorf and Isabel Müller are in hospital at Husum. Bergendorf's fighting for his life but Frau Müller is stable.'

'Dammit.'

'I found incriminating evidence against Bergendorf in his house, though.'

'Found?'

'Lying openly on the table: explicit photographs of children. Very explicit. I need a search warrant for his house.'

'Are you absolutely certain? You know we'll have to present the evidence. Bergendorf is—'

'I realise that, DSU Warnke, but we're running out of time here.'

Warnke said nothing.

'I think it might be a good idea to get the warrant via Flensburg,' Lena said. 'Evidently, Bergendorf's got friends in Kiel.'

'Give me an hour.'

'We also need to issue an information blackout regarding this afternoon's events.'

'That's more difficult.'

'I need forty-eight hours and an armed response unit on Amrum. Tomorrow lunchtime should be early enough.'

'What's your plan?'

Lena took her time before replying. 'Put it this way, you chose to keep one or two details about the case from me. You had your reasons. I trusted you and everything's worked out OK so far. Now it's your turn to trust me. I also have my reasons.'

'How many men?'

'Six. I'm in command.'

'Don't let me down!' said Warnke and hung up.

Lena breathed deeply before ringing Leon back. 'We're good to go. I can be online in ten minutes to call the gentlemen to a meeting.'

'Time?'

'Eight o'clock tonight. I'll log on fifteen minutes early so you can show me the ropes.'

'Just to get this straight, we're actually dealing directly with these filthy bastards who rape little children?'

'It looks that way, Leon.'

'Later,' he said and hung up.

Lena couldn't recall any form of goodbye from Leon in the past. He clearly harboured an intense personal hatred for people who viewed children as livestock and destroyed them mentally and physically. Whatever the case, he seemed intensely motivated.

Lena picked up Bergendorf's laptop and walked over to one of the two young local constables. She'd previously asked him to do as neat a job as possible on the window in the guest bathroom. He'd picked up a pane of glass of the right dimensions from the glazier, removed the remains of the damaged double-glazing, and used putty to fix the new pane in position. If you didn't look too closely, it was hard to tell it apart from the other windows.

'Great work, Constable. That's all for today, thank you. And once again, not a word to anyone about this afternoon.'

Lena had also sworn Dr Neumann to secrecy, telling him it was of the utmost importance for the success of her investigation.

The young man nodded. 'I know.'

'To anyone – not even your nearest and dearest. Got it?'

'Sergeant Reimers . . . ?' he asked hesitantly. 'I . . . We've been wondering what . . . ?'

'I know, and I promise you'll be fully informed in due course. It's not possible just yet.'

Lena locked the door and waited for the young policeman to drive off, then climbed into the Passat and headed back to the house on the beach.

Johann was sitting in the kitchen with a glass of water, staring into space. Lena joined him.

'So that was that then, I guess,' Johann said after a while.

'Was it your first time?'

He nodded.

'You did everything right. If Bergendorf had kept his trap shut, Isabel would have let him go. I had her all buttered up. It was my only chance.'

'Any news from the hospital yet?'

'I've just spoken with one of the local uniforms – they're both in surgery still.' Lena decided to add a little white lie. 'The doctor said it's looking good for Isabel, though.'

'And Bergendorf?'

'Might take a while, but it's not looking too bad now.'

'Are we leaving today? I guess the case is pretty much closed. We can finish off the rest from home, can't we? The internal investigations department will take care of Reimers. Isabel Müller will be off to court, and—'

'Hang on, did I miss something? Didn't our dear Herr Bergendorf have a few friends we were anxious to meet?'

Johann looked up. 'That ship has well and truly sailed now Bergendorf's in hospital. They'll find out in no time and write him off.'

'Fortunately, I've had a word with Warnke. We've got forty-eight hours. Search warrant for his house is on the way.' She pointed to the laptop, which she'd fired up and connected to the Wi-Fi. 'Guess who this belongs to?'

Johann straightened up. 'What are you doing?'

'I'm calling in a chatroom meeting for this evening. I'm going to invite the lovely gentlemen to Amrum.'

'You're going to pretend to be Bergendorf? Why on earth would they come here? They'll never agree to it.'

'Let's wait and see. I'm pretty sure they've been here before enough times. I just need to think up a good reason – or rather, we do.'

Johann seemed to warm to the idea. 'OK, let's think this through. Those guys know the CID is on the island.'

'You're right. They need to think we've left for the mainland – we decided in the end that the death wasn't suspicious, so case closed. They have to reckon there's no risk in them coming.'

'I'm with you so far. But if Lübbers is one of that lot, he'll know, won't he?'

'Not necessarily. For all he knows, we did clear off today. There's no official report through yet from today, and he wouldn't be expecting one in any case if the death has now been classed as natural.'

'OK, that could work. But that's not enough to get them to come here. We need something special, something they can only do here.'

'It has to have something to do with the home.'

'Do you think we could sell the idea that Sabine Bohlen's willing to come to the party? Even though she doesn't know anything about it?'

'Unlikely. And even if she were, why would they have to come here? To sign a contract? No.'

'True,' Johann said.

'Let's take a moment to think. What's the connecting factor with all these men?'

'Their addiction to sexually abusing innocent children. Their lust for power. Plus, it's probably a huge money-maker – several birds with one stone, as it were.'

'OK, so they must need a regular supply of new children – not so easy in this day and age. The only way would be to travel abroad or—'

'—Or to transport the children over here,' Johann said, finishing her thought. 'Put them on the market for a while and then get rid of them again. Similar to forced prostitution.'

'That's right. These gentlemen are far too posh to travel to Thailand, to put themselves in perpetual danger of ending up in a prison they can't simply buy themselves out of. So they need fresh "stock". Bergendorf might just have come across a new supplier.'

'Purely by coincidence and right at this precise moment? They'll never buy it. Those guys must be jumpy as hell.'

'You're right,' Lena said. 'Bergendorf needs to explain how exactly he met this new contact.'

'Bohlen! What about Bohlen? He was under a lot of pressure to pay back the money. Maybe it was his contact? He must have been in on it not too long ago.'

'Yes, that might work. He could've tried to buy his way out of it with a contact.' Lena tried to think how the story might have unfolded. 'Bergendorf kept a low profile while we were on the island, but now we're gone he can finally talk about this new associate from . . .'

'Romania?' suggested Johann.

'Yes. The contact from Romania is getting impatient and wants to seal the deal. But he also wants to speak with the lot of them because he doesn't trust Bergendorf.'

'But isn't the whole idea to deal with as few real contacts as possible? And to conduct business through middlemen who ideally don't even know who the real players are?'

'Probably. So why might the Romanian be wanting to meet them all?' asked Lena.

'It's too big for Bergendorf to handle.'

'Right,' Lena said, thinking it over. 'He doesn't feel he can decide on his own whether the contact is serious. The deal is huge and there's a lot of money at stake. Bergendorf needs their support during negotiations.'

'But I doubt the whole lot will show. We'll be lucky if even one of them turns up – two would be hitting the jackpot.'

'I guess you're right. If I ask for too much they'll get suspicious. OK, let's think up a name for this Romanian.'

'How about Ionescu? I used to know someone from Romania by that name. Sounds authentic enough.'

Lena agreed. They kept working on the story until she felt suf-ficiently comfortable with the web of lies they had created. When she noticed Johann's look of utter exhaustion, she suggested they take a break and he went off to his room.

Meanwhile, Warnke had been granted the search warrant and had emailed it through to Lena. The constable from Husum called to say that Isabel Müller's surgery had gone well and Bergendorf's condition had stabilised once he'd been put in an induced coma.

Lena reached for her phone and rang Leon.

'Nervous?' he asked.

'A little. Let's see how I do "over on the dark side".'

'You'll be even better than usual.'

'Wow! Was that a compliment? I'm flattered.'

Leon laughed. Lena realised she'd never heard him laugh before. 'You should be. It won't be happening again.'

'I don't doubt it. Right, can you help me set up the meeting then?'

They spent the next half-hour in the mysterious world of the Dark Web. Leon wished her good luck before hanging up.

Lena closed the laptop and called Warnke. 'Bergendorf has been a very active chap on the Dark Web, and in one secret chatroom in particular. I was able to recover his last conversation. I've called in a meeting for tonight.'

'Right. Well, I won't ask how you managed all that so quickly, but congratulations. You're going to set a trap?'

'I won't manage to get them all to come to Amrum.'

'You're thinking about a principal witness deal?'

'We'll see who shows up and go from there.'

'Let me know straight away how it goes, won't you? I wish you luck, Lena – you're going to need it.'

'Luck?' Lena muttered after she'd hung up. 'I don't think that'll be enough to pull this thing off . . .'

Her phone buzzed. A text. Lena read it and couldn't help but smile at Erck's message:

I'm available if you need a break from chasing criminals? X

She typed a reply and pressed send:

Criminals never rest. Call you later x

She looked at the clock. One hour to go until they found out if the case was closed or if Hein Bohlen's death had brought about some measure of good. Perhaps it was a way for him to posthumously atone for a small part of his guilt. Lena got up and opened the kitchen window to let in the fresh, salty breeze. She closed her eyes and inhaled deeply.

Johann and Lena sat side by side. They'd entered the Dark Web shortly before eight and logged into the chatroom. It was a waiting game now.

One after the other, the names lit up until 'Schwarz' arrived and started typing.

> Schwarz: Looks like most of us could make it in spite of the short notice. Let's wait another 5 minutes in case Weiss turns up.

> Weiss: Apologies. I'm here now. Had appointments.

> Schwarz: I declare the meeting open. Over to you, Berg.

> Berg: I'm sorry we had to meet again so soon, but we have an important decision to make. The good news first: the CID has left the island. And I also

have it on good authority that the death is no longer regarded as suspicious.

Schwarz: Interesting. I hadn't heard yet. Very well – that's one less thing to worry about. But that's not why you called the meeting. Why are we here?

Berg: At my last meeting with HB, he offered an alternative means of repayment: a promising contact from Romania. I didn't think much of it, to be honest, but then yesterday the man turns up on my doorstep.

Rose: Get to the point. What's this all about?

Berg: Steady on! I wouldn't have bothered you if it wasn't important.

Beil: We're waiting!!

Berg: He's offering excellent stock from Romania and Belarus at a highly competitive price.

Schwarz: How can you tell?

Berg: He had photos. Good photos. He'd organise freight both ways. We'd pick and choose from a catalogue, delivery within the week.

Rose: Cost?

Berg: As I said, highly competitive. If the boys are only half as good as in the pictures . . .

Schwarz: Chatroom protocol, please.

Berg: Sorry. The stock looks excellent. Though I wouldn't want to stick my neck out for this Romanian.

Weiss: I think it sounds good. How are we supposed to close the deal, Berg?

Schwarz: We need to be absolutely certain. How do we know who's behind this guy?

Weiss: Berg would've already checked him out?

Berg: As far as I could at short notice. Looks clean.

Weiss: Told you it sounds good.

Schwarz: Since when are you so happy to take a risk?

Weiss: I'm not, but I trust Berg. Don't you?

Beil: Of course we do. That's one of our founding principles. Well, Berg, what's the next step?

Berg: We're talking a rather large sum. I don't want to decide on my own.

Schwarz: Let him make us an offer, the usual way. Then we'll see.

Berg: That's just the problem. He's only here for two more days and wants the deal done and dusted. He's coming back tomorrow at 7 p.m.

Schwarz: Strange way of conducting business.

Weiss: Snap out of it, Schwarz. What do you need, Berg?

Berg: I need on-site support. Can anyone get here tomorrow and help me check it out?

Weiss: Would if I could, but I'm in Barcelona with meetings I can't cancel. What about you, Schwarz? And Beil? You've got plenty of spare time, haven't you?

Schwarz: This is happening way too fast. We need to slow things down.

Berg: That's what I told the Romanian, but he wasn't interested. I think he's got other interested parties besides us.

Weiss: Beil, are you in?

Beil: If I must. But not on my own.

Weiss: Schwarz?

Schwarz: Do we have all the facts in place?

Berg: Yes, as far as I can tell. We could close the deal tomorrow. The Romanian is definitely a professional. I could tell.

Schwarz: Fair enough, but I only hope you're right. It's quite a hassle to organise.

Berg: Trust me! I wouldn't have asked you if I didn't think it was worth it.

Rose: So that's it for now? Report back to the rest of us ASAP. You three have full authority to close the deal. Anyone not in favour?

Schwarz: Looks like we're agreed. I'm calling the meeting closed.

Lena breathed a sigh of relief as the last user logged off. She hadn't thought it would be this easy. Luckily, 'Weiss' had supported her. Her phone buzzed and she checked the display. Leon.

You were good. Congratulations. I wasn't too bad either, was I?

Lena grinned. Evidently, 'Weiss' hadn't been able to make it and Leon had taken his place.

22

Erck knocked against the side of the beach chair. 'Room for a little one?'

Lena moved to the side and lifted her blanket. 'Don't take up all the space, will you?'

Erck leaned down to kiss her. 'I've never needed a lot of room.'

Lena pulled him down beside her. 'How was your day?'

'Probably not as interesting as yours.'

Aside from managing holiday homes, Erck also set up websites for his clients and, where necessary, fixed leaky pipes or broken heaters.

'You might well be right about today, but I also spend plenty of time at my desk writing reports and researching boring stuff.'

'So you caught the crooks then? I heard the air ambulance come twice.'

Lena held her index finger to her lips. 'Let's keep that for another time.' She pulled a bottle of white wine from a pocket in the beach chair and handed Erck a glass.

'What are we toasting?' he asked once their glasses were filled.

'To the fact that I feel so wonderfully comfortable around you,' Lena said with a smile.

'Sounds marvellous! And ditto.'

She raised her glass and chinked it against his. 'We're in agreement then.'

He took a sip. 'Haven't we always been – most of the time?'

'Sometimes ninety-nine per cent is just not enough.'

'I hate that one per cent with all my heart.'

Lena kissed his lips. 'My hero. Let's forget everything for tonight. Promise?'

He nodded. 'For the rest of our lives is fine by me too.'

Dawn was breaking outside. Lena had woken a few minutes earlier and stood gazing at the sky out of Erck's bedroom window.

'Was that our last night together?' Erck asked quietly behind her.

'I thought you were still asleep.'

'Is that your reply?'

Lena turned to him. 'Would you want a long-distance relationship?'

'I don't work much in winter. I could come over to Kiel.'

'And the other eight months?'

'Don't you have a branch in Husum or something?'

'Not really.'

'Is Kiel that important to you?'

'Not really.'

'Can't you become a fisherwoman or a doctor or something? God, I don't know . . .' Erck swallowed. 'Who on earth would think of doing such a crazy job?'

'I like it and it suits me. You know that.'

'Will I see you again?'

'Do you want to?'

'Would I ask if I didn't?'

'Can you give me some time?'

'More time?'

Lena said nothing. Why was she here, in fact? Hadn't she known there'd be no simple hello and goodbye with Erck? He wasn't the type for a one-night stand. He'd been her first true love. True love – hadn't she always hated that kind of sentimental bullshit? Pure imagination, an absolute pack of lies.

'You'd soon hate me and curse me and—'

'Why don't you let that be my problem? You're an adult, I'm an adult. Nothing else matters.'

'Can you please just hold me?'

Erck pulled her into his arms and kissed her.

'Morning,' Johann said when Lena walked into the kitchen. 'I hope you didn't fall asleep in that beach chair?'

'Morning! Nope, I'm about twenty years too old for that. Any news?'

'I rang the hospital. Isabel Müller is stable. The DNA result from the clothing is in. As we thought: Bergendorf. He and Bohlen must've had an argument on the day Bohlen died. A pretty bad argument, I'd say – at least a scuffle, if not more. I'm guessing Bergendorf came off second best. Hein Bohlen was at least a head taller than him, not to mention stronger.'

'Maybe that explains Bohlen's desperation. If he really went for Bergendorf, he must have known the banker would land him in deep trouble – that's why he hardly showed his face at the children's home that day and quickly went out on his usual night-time walk.'

'Bergendorf's still in an induced coma. They don't know if he'll make it.'

'Can Isabel Müller be interviewed yet?'

'Yes, the doctor said that would be fine.'

Lena grabbed the ferry timetable. 'Next ferry goes in twenty minutes. We can be back this afternoon in time to meet the special unit.'

Johann stood up and grinned. 'Bugger. I was hoping for the helicopter.'

'Hello, Frau Müller,' Lena said.

'Don't waste your breath. I'm not talking to you.'

Isabel Müller lay in a single-bed room with a policeman standing guard outside her door and a policewoman inside with her. Her right shoulder was heavily bandaged and her face looked drawn, with dark shadows under her eyes.

Lena asked the young policewoman to leave them for a while. At Lena's signal, Johann also left the room.

'It's important you understand that I'm only going to say this once. If you don't talk, you've missed your chance.' Lena waited until Isabel gave an almost imperceptible nod. 'I'm a policewoman and it was my duty to try to save Bergendorf's life. Believe me when I say it wasn't easy. Everything I told you was more or less the truth. We're on to those men and I'm doing everything in my power to catch them. Do you follow?' Isabel Müller nodded again. 'Bergendorf's in a coma and we don't know if he'll make it. I'm not supposed to tell you this, but I'm making an exception. If we can't get at those men through Bergendorf we have to find another way. I know you swapped Bohlen's medication and we can prove it. You were hoping he'd have a heart attack. You'll be questioned on the matter and on your attack on Bergendorf at a later stage. Right now I'm interested in anything you might know about these men. Do you have any idea as to their identities? How did you find out about Bergendorf? What happened to your brother? Did he give you any names?'

At last Isabel Müller began to talk, haltingly. Her brother had first tried to kill himself at fourteen and was repeatedly placed in psychiatric-care settings. His feelings of guilt and shame had prevented him from opening up. Not even the psychologists had managed to get through to him. Florian only started disclosing details from the past to his sister shortly before his suicide in Oldenburg. She'd started her research once she'd recovered from the initial shock. Hein Bohlen was the first man she'd identified, but according to her brother he hadn't taken part in the sexual abuse itself. Apparently, he was responsible for picking out the boys and keeping them in check. She didn't find out anything else until after Florian's death, when she'd found the diaries he'd kept during his time at the different children's homes. From Florian's detailed descriptions of the men who raped him, she'd identified five different individuals.

When she realised she wasn't getting anywhere with her research, she'd decided to go for a job at the home on Amrum. Anna Bauer had rapidly agreed to leave the island when she heard what kind of dealings Hein Bohlen was involved in. The twenty thousand euros Isabel paid her had certainly helped too – the money came from the pay-out of her brother's life insurance. With the information Anna Bauer had given her, Isabel had found it easy to convince Hein Bohlen and his wife that she was the right person for the job. When she realised that Bohlen hadn't been part of the gang's criminal activities in years, she'd started sleeping with him in the hope of extracting more information. The only thing she'd found out was that Bergendorf was putting pressure on Bohlen. Comparing Bergendorf with her brother's notes, she became convinced he was one of the men in the trafficking ring. She'd come up with the plan to kill Bohlen by reducing his beta blockers at around the same time. The licence plate number Isabel had given the detectives belonged to a vehicle she'd noted down during a surveillance session on Bergendorf's property.

'I was hoping you'd find those bastards,' Isabel said at the end of her report.

'I need your brother's diaries. They weren't in your room.'

'I stored a few boxes at a friend's place in Hamburg – they're in with that stuff. And the list I created is on my laptop.' She told Lena the file's name and location.

Lena rose to her feet.

'Will you catch them?' Isabel asked. Lena could tell how draining the last half-hour had been for the young woman.

'I certainly hope so – if not today, then very soon.'

'Thanks. If you do, it's all been worth it.'

◆ ◆ ◆

Lena filled Johann in on their drive back to Dagebüll. On the ferry, they stood in silence for a long time, enjoying the view from the top deck.

'So what's the plan for this evening?' Johann asked eventually.

'I assume that one of the two gentlemen will be Chief Prosecutor Lübbers. He knows me, so it'd be good if you could receive him and lead him into the house. Just tell him you're Bergendorf's new assistant.'

'No problem.'

'We'll question the two men separately. One of them's got to crack before they get to talk to their lawyers. I've been authorised to offer a deal.'

'It might just work. You'll take on the chief prosecutor, right?'

Lena nodded and gazed out over the water. Erck popped into her mind. Had the last few days on the island changed something for her? She forced the thought aside and suggested to Johann that they find a quiet spot on the ship to discuss their strategy for the evening.

23

Lena positioned two officers from the armed response unit some distance away from the driveway to the mansion while the remaining four waited in the kitchen. They'd arrived on the island in two vehicles which were now parked, well camouflaged, not far from the house. Lena had decided against surveillance of the ferry to avoid any unnecessary risk. The doorbell rang the first time just after six. Johann opened. A short, thickset man stood in front of him.

'Good evening,' said Johann. 'I'm Johann, Herr Bergendorf's assistant.'

'Ramke,' said the man. 'So old Bergendorf's got a butler now? Fancy that.'

'Would you care to follow me to the library?' asked Johann.

The man handed his coat to Johann, then headed towards the library without paying any further attention to the detective sergeant. Lena, who'd been waiting around the corner, followed him into the room.

'Oh, more staff?'

Lena pulled the door shut behind her, took her police pass from her pocket and handed it to the man. 'So to speak, except that I'm paid by the state.'

The man stared at her photocard. 'Is this some kind of a joke? Where's Bergendorf?' He came across as aggressive but a touch uncertain.

'Unfortunately, Herr Bergendorf can't make it. Are you carrying any form of ID?'

The man threw Lena's pass aside. 'What's the meaning of this?' he yelled. His eyes were darting around in rising panic. 'Bergendorf, enough is enough!'

Lena picked up her pass, glared at him and shouted, 'Sit down! Now.' The man scowled at her but did as she asked. 'ID, please.'

When the man didn't react, Lena opened the door. 'Come in!'

Two officers clad in black came into the room and positioned themselves next to Lena. 'It's your choice. Show me your ID or I'll have you arrested on the spot.'

The man swallowed and reached into his back pocket to pull out his wallet, then placed his ID card on the table. Lena glanced at the name and handed the card to one of the officers.

'Thank you. I think I can manage on my own from here.'

Once they'd left the room, Lena joined her suspect at the table. 'Alois Ramke?' The man nodded. 'Hand over your phone, please.'

The man reluctantly reached into his pocket again and passed Lena his mobile.

'I'll get straight to the point. You're under suspicion of being a member of a group that has been engaging in organised child trafficking and sexual abuse of minors for over a decade. We have evidence that you have personally taken part in at least one rape of a minor. I don't doubt for a second that we'll be able to prove many more such cases during the course of our investigation.'

'I want to talk to my lawyer.'

'You have the right to remain silent, and yes, you'll get the chance to contact your lawyer. But first of all, I'll have to transfer you to Kiel, where you'll be presented before the judge.'

Alois Ramke said nothing.

Lena slid the two chatroom transcripts across the table for him to see.

'I'm guessing you're "Beil". Your house will be searched within the next two hours, but as far as I can see, we've already got more than enough to put you behind bars for many, many years.'

'What do you want from me?'

'I have been authorised to offer you a principal witness deal. The offer stands from now for' – she checked the time – 'fifteen minutes exactly.' Lena set the timer on her phone and placed it on the desk in front of Ramke.

She could tell the man was struggling. His breathing was shallow, his eyes flickered nervously and the colour of his face changed from red to chalky white. Finally, he pressed the stop button on Lena's phone and said, 'I won't say another word. I want to talk to my lawyer.'

Lena picked up her phone and the chatroom transcripts. 'Your call.' She opened the door and waved the two armed response officers back into the room.

'Well?' asked Johann, who was waiting in the hallway for the next visitor to arrive.

'He's refusing to talk. He's not interested in a deal. I've a feeling he's not privy to everything going on in that group, but you may have more luck with him.'

Lena's phone buzzed: a text from one of the officers stationed outside. 'Number two's on his way. Take him to the living room this time.'

Johann grinned. 'At your command, ma'am.'

Moments later the doorbell rang. As before, Johann introduced himself as Bergendorf's assistant and led the tall, blond man into the living room, where Lena was now waiting.

'Evening, Chief Prosecutor Lübbers,' she said in greeting.

Lübbers stared at Lena, half-turned as if sizing up his chances of making a run for it, but then turned back to her. 'Have we met before?'

'I don't know if you know me.' Lena stepped towards him, holding out her police pass. He glanced at it and asked, 'What are you doing here? As far as I know, this is still the private domicile of my friend Herr Bergendorf. Show me the search warrant!'

'Why don't we sit down? This conversation may take a while.'

'No, it won't. Where's Bergendorf?' Lübbers spoke in the arrogant tone favoured by a superior when dealing with a seemingly incompetent subordinate. 'I'm leaving now. I doubt you'll have a job to go to in the morning.'

He turned round and opened the door, slowly closing it again when he saw the two armed officers waiting outside. 'Are you quite out of your mind? Does your boss have any idea what you're up to?'

'Would you please give me your phone?' Lena held out her hand. 'It'll be easier for you if you cooperate,' she added with a glance at the door.

'Under protest. I demand to know what's going on.'

'Please, sit down,' said Lena.

'I promise you'll regret this.'

He took his coat off and folded it carefully before taking a seat. Lena placed the two chatroom transcripts on the table in front of him and waited for him to scan the text.

'What's all this?' he snarled.

'We're questioning Herr Ramke in the next room. It's only a matter of time until he accepts our principal witness deal. I'll leave you for a moment.' She stood up, opened the door and let the two officers in. 'These gentlemen will look after you in the meantime.'

She went to the kitchen, rang Warnke and gave him Alois Ramke's details.

'And number two is Chief Prosecutor Lübbers.'

'I'll order search warrants for them both. The chatroom transcripts and their presence alone should suffice.'

'I'll be in touch when there's news.'

'Please do.'

Lena returned to the living room and waited until the two policemen had left the room.

'How much longer is this going to take?' asked Lübbers. 'I don't need to explain to you how many laws you've breached already.'

'Herr Lübbers, I'm placing you under arrest.' She informed him of his rights and asked, 'Can we talk properly now? You know precisely how this works. Right this minute, search warrants are being issued for your house and your office. My colleagues will start sifting through your things in half an hour at the most.'

'You are completely and utterly insane. I'm going to sue the living daylights out of you. You do realise your time as a police officer is over, don't you? You can consider yourself lucky if you don't end up in prison for this.'

'Herr Lübbers,' Lena said calmly but sternly, 'as with your colleague, I've been authorised also to offer you a principal witness deal, provided you have the information we need. The chat shows clearly that you hold a leading position within your group.'

'You're mad!'

'And you're a fucking paedophile!' shouted Lena angrily. 'It's over! Grab this one last chance, or forget it. We'll bring you to book for every last crime you've ever committed. You'll be sent down for a very long time. You do realise who you'll meet in there, don't you, because I do.'

'You honestly believe you can pressure me with this ridiculous little show of yours? It's nothing but hot air.'

Lena's phone buzzed. She checked the display and smiled. 'Oh well, it's your life. One of my colleagues has been inside for a year now. I'm sure you'll have heard about him. He took bribes, manipulated witness statements and leaked confidential information. He's in Flensburg Prison to minimise the chances of bumping into inmates he's put there himself, but he barely survived the last attack. Shall I tell you what they did to him?'

Her phone buzzed again. She read the message, stood up and walked to the door. 'Terrific. Your friend Ramke wants to speak with me. I'll be right back.'

She met Johann in the hallway. They'd arranged the text messages beforehand. 'Did you get anywhere?'

'No, not a sausage. He's absolutely convinced we can't touch him, though he did look a bit anxious when I left the room just now.'

'Lübbers didn't. Maybe Ramke will cave first after all.'

'How far are we going to take this?'

'The whole night if we have to. We need a result.'

'OK, back into the fray.'

Back in the living room, Lena sat down with Chief Prosecutor Lübbers and waited. After ten minutes of mutual silence, the blond man cleared his throat. 'So, where do we go from here, Inspector?'

'We wait.'

'If you'd be so kind as to tell me what for.'

'My team have brought their vehicles over. The next ferry doesn't leave for a while.'

'What exactly are you accusing me of? Visiting a friend on Amrum? You can't be serious.'

Finally, Lena thought, but didn't let it show. 'When did you last speak with your friend?'

'Yesterday. We arranged a meeting.'

'What time, roughly?'

'Late afternoon, I think.'

'You can't be talking about Herr Bergendorf. He was in an induced coma by then.'

Lübbers swallowed. 'That can't be right.'

'I'm sorry you didn't hear about it. Fresh findings not released in the public domain – you know what that means.'

She pulled the search warrant from her pocket and placed it on the table in front of Lübbers. 'Not that it's any of your business, but since you asked so nicely . . .'

Lübbers checked the document then pushed it away.

'I took the liberty of taking part in your little chat last night. I borrowed your friend's name. Not very imaginative, I must say.'

'That was you?' Lübbers looked irritated.

'You didn't think we could do it? It wasn't that hard to find you lot on the Dark Web.'

'I don't believe you. You're bluffing.'

'Well, there is no Romanian. And Hein Bohlen did not die of natural causes. And you're not the saint you make yourself out to be either.'

Lübbers said nothing.

'Remember Osnabrück? A boy named Florian Müller – or did you just call the children by a number? A small, skinny boy with blond hair. Don't remember? He remembered every last detail. He described each one of you so well that I recognised Herr Ramke immediately.'

Still Lübbers remained silent.

'You know what? The first witness is always the hardest to find in cases like this. But once one talks, everyone else follows. Right now an experienced team of investigators is scouring children's homes up and down the country on the lookout for further victims. It's only a matter of time until—'

'Won't you just quit this nonsense!' exclaimed Lübbers.

'You do know the difference between going straight to jail or accepting a principal witness deal, don't you? The former means a life of hell; the latter means that life goes on for you. You'll lose your job, of course, and you'll have to move, start over. It'll be tough, really tough. But you'll live. You won't be able to practise as a lawyer any more, but you'll get a second chance. How old are you now? Mid-fifties? Let's say a fifteen-year jail term – that would make you seventy when you came out. Well, always provided that you survive that hell on earth.'

Lena's phone buzzed again. She checked the display, rose to her feet and said, 'I'll be right back.'

'Any progress?' asked Johann, handing her a cup of coffee.

'Not really. You?'

'I feel like he's beginning to crack. I can't promise anything, though.'

'Dammit. The moment they get to their lawyers tomorrow they won't say another word. I'm not even sure what the judge will say then: two respectable citizens, blah blah blah.'

'We've still got a few hours left,' Johann said. 'I'll go and tighten the thumbscrews.'

Lena nodded and went back in.

'So what now?' said Lübbers, still playing confident. 'You're going to tell me again that Ramke's about to talk?' He gave a short laugh.

Lena waited a few minutes before she spoke again. 'Have you ever thought about what you're doing to those children? You were a boy once.' She looked at Lübbers intently. 'Those big hands groping you everywhere, touching you in places only your mother's touched you at bathtime. You're scared, so terribly scared, of having done something wrong and getting punished for it. You're ashamed and you hate yourself for what's happening. You can't sleep at night because you're terrified someone will come and grab you, drag you back to hell, back into that black hole you'll never ever be able to forget.'

Lübbers swallowed. For the first time her words seemed to affect him.

'You cry all night until your eyes hurt. You can't breathe. You run to the window and open it, but you still feel like you're suffocating. Your whole body aches. You stare at your hands but don't know if they're yours. A noise. You flinch. Is that him? Is he coming back to get you? What's he going to ask of you this time? It hurts so much, so horribly much. Why isn't anyone helping you? You want to die. You find a knife, but it's not sharp enough. Hell is black and silent. No one hears you when you scream. No one.' Lena stared at Lübbers for a while before she went on. 'Believe you me, you won't fare any better in prison. The only difference is that you'll deserve what those brutal men will do to you. Every day, in the shower, in a dark corner of the laundry, at night when the warden accidentally forgets to lock your cell. It'll be a never-ending nightmare. Your nightmare.'

'What do you want from me?' asked Lübbers in a whisper.

Lena sensed he was about to crack. 'I want it to stop. As of today. If you have an ounce of decency left in you, you start talking now. I guarantee you'll get a deal. A child rapist in gaol – you might as well hang yourself now. And believe me, I'll personally make sure the inmates hear who's sharing their cell. You won't even make it through to your trial.'

'What guarantees do I get?' Lübbers seemed broken. He was staring down at his trembling hands, his face ashen.

'You give me the names of the two remaining chatroom participants, then I call the attorney general and you have a chat with him. Then we'll keep going until we've gathered all the most important details – dates, names, places.'

'How do I know you're not tricking me?' he asked weakly.

'I won't record our conversation. Today, it's just you and me. You can deny everything tomorrow. Your word against mine. In the morning, we go to Kiel and we settle the deal there. You'll be taken straight to a safehouse, where you'll be guarded until your trial date. You know the procedure.'

Lübbers closed his eyes for a moment. Then he opened them and spoke. 'Martin Woltershausen, Münster, chairman of Maschen Incorporated. Jürgen Wiesner, Hanover, member of the local parliament.'

Lena noted down the names and stood up with her phone in her hand. 'I'll be right back.'

Epilogue

Lena stood at the railing with her face turned towards the sunshine. The ferry left the terminal and gradually gained speed.

The last two weeks had been hard work. A thirty-strong special commission had picked up where she had left off. Twenty-two men had been arrested so far. Bergendorf had survived and would be transferred to prison in around a week. He'd shown little emotion when Lena interrogated him. The only time he'd looked a tad insecure was when he heard that Lübbers had confessed everything, sung like a veritable canary, but he soon regained the cockiness he'd been practising for decades and refused to make any further statement. Lena felt certain that even the most senior prosecutors would find him a tough nut.

The attorney general was preparing one of the biggest trials Kiel had seen in decades. The media response had been huge, with new reports still coming in daily.

The special commission would work on this for months to come. Experts on child abuse cases had been called in from all constabularies in Schleswig-Holstein, together with special investigators from the Federal Criminal Investigation Department. They would carefully check out thousands of leads and interview hundreds of witnesses. Lena had already written countless reports and – at her own request – taken part in the interviews of all the core members of the child-trafficking ring. The extensive confession of the now ex-Chief Prosecutor Lübbers helped the investigators target their activities to force suspects into a corner. House searches, which had taken place simultaneously right across Germany, had produced irrefutable evidence. The attorney general was convinced they'd busted an international ring of child traffickers and that many more investigations and trials would now ensue worldwide. Everyone was aware that this job could stretch on for years and that despite the diligence of the investigators, some of the criminals would still manage to evade justice.

Lena's conversation with DSU Warnke had lasted only ten minutes. He had congratulated her, while she had asked for two things: a week off, and for four colleagues to assist her in reopening the case of the missing boy from the Lübeck area. Warnke had given her two weeks for the investigation and said she needed to come back with new evidence.

Once Reimers had sent in the note in support of his sick leave, he was questioned at the clinic where he'd been staying and then admitted to having informed Bergendorf about Hein Bohlen's death. When he confessed to other dealings with the criminal gang, he was suspended from his job and was also now awaiting trial.

Isabel Müller had been taken into custody on her release from hospital. She'd admitted to swapping the medication and was awaiting trial for this, as well as for attacking Herbert Bergendorf. Lena felt sure that the judge would consider her personal history and that of her brother as mitigating circumstances, but she wasn't sure if Isabel would get away with probation rather than a custodial sentence. Lena had spoken with the prosecutor in charge of Isabel's case and urged him to place her under compulsory psychiatric care where she could access the therapy she needed.

◆ ◆ ◆

The last few clouds in the sky had burned off. Lena took out her phone and called the familiar number. Erck picked up after the second ring.

'And there was I, beginning to think you'd forgotten all about me. Not much fun only being able to read about you in the news.'

'OK, well, how are you fixed over the next six days?'

'Are those seagulls I hear in the background?'

'Could be.'

'The next six days, you said? Hmm, I'm not sure – let me just check my diary. Oh look, that's weird – absolutely nothing over the next six days. I've never had that happen before.'

'I missed you.'

'Not half as much as I missed you.'

'You can tell me all about it in a couple of hours. I bought a bottle of wine.'

'And I've got the key to the beach chair.'

'You seriously never gave it back?'

'Did you think I was joking?'

'No, not really.'

'Lena?'

'I'm still here!'

'You'd better get a move on!'

'I've got blue lights and a siren.'

'That's good.'

'See you in a bit, Erck.'

'See you in a bit, Lena.'

ABOUT THE AUTHOR

Anna Johannsen has lived in Northern Friesland since her childhood. She loves the landscape and the people of the region and is especially fond of the North Frisian islands that provide the setting for her Island Mystery novels starring DI Lena Lorenzen. *The Body on the Beach* is a #1 Kindle bestseller.

ABOUT THE TRANSLATOR

Photo © 2017 Danice Hamilton

Lisa Reinhardt studied English and linguistics at the University of Otago and lives with her family in rural New Zealand.